"I was wondering if our fight was over," Jamie mused, as he hooked one finger under the gold chain around her neck with the pretense of adjusting it, and allowed his other fingers to brush the soft warm skin beneath.

Mary gave a deep, despairing sigh. "Yes, I suppose it is. But only because you seem to have gotten your own way, as usual."

"It's not official until we kiss and make up," he informed her solemnly, pulling at the chain to draw her closer.

Her lips parted and her arms slipped around his waist as he folded her into his arms. They held each other until, reluctantly, he raised his head. "I can't let you have your own way," he groaned against her forehead, "because you want to do crazy things like leave me, and I can't permit that. You belong to me again and I'll never let you go."

ABOUT THE AUTHOR

Marie Ziobro was a voracious reader of romances before ever trying to write one. But as she found herself reworking her favorite stories in her own mind more and more often, she finally decided to sit down and write one herself. Marie lives in Florida and works for NASA at the Kennedy Space Center.

Strange Bedfellows

MARIE ZIOBRO

Harlequin Books

TORONTO • NEW YORK • LONDON
AMSTERDAM • PARIS • SYDNEY • HAMBURG
STOCKHOLM • ATHENS • TOKYO • MILAN

To the men in my life—
and the women in theirs—
with much love.

Published June 1984

First printing April 1984

ISBN 0-373-16059-3

Chapter One

When she allowed herself to think of him at all, Mary remembered their last day together, when they swam naked in the clear blue water of their swimming pool and then made love. It had been the happiest and the saddest day of her life, and she had not seen him again in all the long, lonely four years that had passed since that day. That was why, as she lay in her hospital bed, floating in and out of delirium, Mary knew that she could not be seeing him now.

She tried to gather her scattered senses together and bring the situation into focus, but the pain in her hands was so agonizing that she could think of nothing else. At last, mercifully, someone gave her a shot to ease the pain, but this only compounded the fuzziness in her mind and sent her back into the half-dream state again where she saw things that could not possibly be there.

Vaguely Mary remembered that there had been a fire in her apartment building, and that the little boy upstairs had been alone because his mother had run to the store and had asked Mary to look in on him if he cried. It wasn't clear in her mind how it happened, but the boy had been screaming, and when she ran up to his apartment, there was a circle of flames around his crib. Desperately she had pulled a heavy drapery from one of the windows to beat out the flames and reach the child.

"Cal," she screamed, her harsh voice echoing in the quiet hospital room. "Cal." A shadowy figure hovered over her and gave her another injection that made her mind go fuzzy again, but not before she remembered sleepily that Cal had not been that boy's name at all. Cal was her own little boy—except that he wasn't hers anymore; he was Jamie's. She had no one. And if that was Jamie sitting by her bed scowling, he needn't worry, because she wouldn't call for Cal again.

Mary drifted off to sleep and when she awoke, the chair beside her bed was empty, so that she knew that it had all been part of her nightmare. There was no way Jamie could have found her here, even if, after four years, he had cared enough to look. The last place he would look would be a hospital.

A hospital. Her mind tried wearily to straighten out the sequence of events that had led her here. The little boy—she did not even know his name—had she been in time? Huskily she forced that question past her burned lungs.

"Skipper is going to be just fine, Mrs. Fitzhugh. You're much the worse for wear than he is. You're both fortunate that the firemen arrived when they did."

"Could I...have a glass...water," she managed to get past her parched throat. Instantly she felt strong hands lifting her shoulders, raising her head so that she could sip from the straw that was in the glass being held to her lips. She wondered curiously who was holding her, but her head felt too heavy to turn around and look. Stan was far away in Europe; still, he might have come back because of the accident. She had no idea of how much time had elapsed. "Stash?" she asked tentatively, reverting to her childhood name for him. Oh, if only he were here, she knew everything would be all right.

The fingers that had been holding her shoulders tenderly bit into her skin, and the voice that answered was the one in all the world that she did not want to hear. "Sorry, Manya." The anger in the voice made her wince. "Your boyfriend isn't here. I'm afraid you'll have to settle for your husband."

She forced herself to turn in the direction of that forbidding voice and flinched under the contempt that flowed from those cold gray eyes into her own. "My God," she whispered to herself, "I wasn't dreaming." But before she could pursue this unexpected turn of events, the drugs took effect and she drifted off to sleep.

It was dark when she awoke again, the throbbing pain in her hands forcing her to consciousness. She could see the dark shadowed form of someone sitting by her bed. Jamie? Perhaps if he did not hate her too much, he would help her. Her throat was raw and aching and her body refused to obey her commands to stop the pain from shooting up one leg and through both hands. She turned imploringly toward that implacable shadow. "I hurt," she sobbed, "make it go away."

The shadow at her bedside rose and disappeared, returning almost instantly with a woman in a white uniform who administered an injection with practiced efficiency. Mary breathed a long, shuddering sign of relief as the pain began to ebb.

The shadow at her bedside flung himself across her prone figure, burying his wet face against her throat. "Oh, Manya, Manya. We had it all. Why did you have to ruin it?" She felt his body shaking against her own and she thought wonderingly that he was hurting as much as she was. She raised a heavily bandaged hand helplessly and brought it down gingerly on his shoulder. "Everything will be all right," she promised those shaking shoulders, "everything will be all right." Then she slept again, to dream of happier days when she had once run naked through the grass. . . .

Remembering was always the same. She was lying on the grass asleep, the even tan of her naked body giving mute evidence that she often bared her skin to the sun. Cool water, falling on the sunbaked, oiled skin of her face and breasts, awakened her rudely and she opened startled blue eyes to gaze into Jamie's angry gray ones.

"What the hell are you doing, lying around like that, without a stitch of clothes on?" His voice was thick with anger and something else, which she recognized at once.

She gave him an impudent smile and stretched seductively in the sweet-smelling summer grass, making no effort to rise or cover herself. Her round, full breasts peaked to taut rosy nipples as he watched in fascination. It was just past noon and the sun was August hot. Her bare skin glowed golden in its heat, while Jamie stood and sweltered in a three-piece Brooks Brothers suit, a bulging briefcase tucked under his arm.

His discomfort in the heat brought a sharp edge to his voice. "Damn it, Manya, suppose someone came along and saw you like this!"

Even when he was angry with her, Jamie was so handsome, he made Mary's breath catch in her throat. Towering six feet two over her prone body, his features shadowed by the sun at his back, she had no trouble recalling every familiar line: how his sand-brown hair curled at the nape of his neck; how gray his eyes were; how straight the long line of his nose, which dominated his face; how forbidding the stubborn butt of his chin; and how betraying his warm wide mouth with its sensual lower lip. She loved everything about him and she was far too confident of his own love to be intimidated by his cross words.

"Pooh," she retorted, "there's no one to see. My goodness, there's a ten-foot hedge around the entire property, the gardener doesn't come until tomorrow, Mrs. Barnes has gone shopping for the groceries, and Barbara just picked up Cal to take him over to see your father. We're quite alone," she added impishly as she held out a lazy hand for him to help her up.

"Damn it, Manya, when I come home for lunch, how do you think I feel finding you naked as a jaybird in the grass?"

"Hot!" she teased in a double entendre, and then gave an impatient sigh. "I love you, James Calhoun Fitzhugh Junior, but you'll have to admit you can be very pompous when you want to be." And with that she carefully plucked the briefcase out of his hand and then pushed him, fully dressed, into the pool.

She watched him sink to the bottom and rise, sputtering and spewing water. "You go too far," he threatened. "When the hell are you going to grow up and act like a proper wife and mother?"

She threw her head back in laughter, her pale blond hair coming alive as the sun darted through its waist-length strands. Her eyes, bluer than the brilliant sky overhead, danced with tears of merriment. "I'm ready to be a proper wife whenever you say," she said, giggling.

The frown he had been struggling to keep on his face dissolved into a sensuous grin he could not suppress. "Well, then, damn it, get into this pool and help me out of these wet clothes."

Mary arched her body into the pool in a single sideward motion of fluid grace. Staying underwater, she came up beneath him and tugged off his shoes and socks, surfaced with them, and threw them onto the nearby grass. At the same time he slipped off his coat and unknotted his tie impatiently, flinging them out of the pool and following them with his shirt.

They were both treading water now, facing each

other, her hands undoing his belt buckle with an ease made sure with practice. Jamie's hand reached deep into the pocket of his slacks and retrieved a soggy alligator wallet before she deftly removed his slacks and briefs in one quick motion.

"You've probably ruined my wallet," he complained in a husky whisper as his lips brushed hers.

She took the wallet from him and flipped it expertly to land beside his briefcase. "I'll get you another," she promised as her arms tightened around his waist, locking their bodies together, "and I'll fill it with lots of new Fitzhugh money. Will that make you happy?" Her sky-blue eyes darkened as she gazed up into the crystal-clear gray of his.

"You know what makes me happy." His body came to life against her own. "But we can't keep meeting like this"—he laughed—"it's costing me a fortune in suits." His mouth found hers hungrily and drew the breath from her body as his hands restaked their possession of her body.

When he allowed her to breathe, she laughed in his ear. "I thought you wanted lunch," she teased, pretending to pull away from the urgent demand of his body. His arms tightened almost cruelly in his determination to hold her fast.

"You know what I want," he muttered. "God, it seems like hours since I last held you like this."

"Six o'clock this morning, to be exact," she answered primly, "and midnight before that. Really, Jamie, old married folks with a three-year-old child simply cannot continue to make love three times a day!"

His hands were driving her crazy and he knew it. "You're right," he surprised her by agreeing, although the glint in his eyes should have warned her. "I keep telling you that four times would be much more practical—before meals and at bedtime." And with that his mouth claimed possession of hers as he pulled her under the water that their twisting bodies had churned up.

She writhed against him, protesting her lack of oxygen, even as her body flamed under his. Twisting her legs around his, she kicked them both back to the surface. "You'll drown me," she protested in mock exasperation.

He responded with a quick grin. "You're right again. I'll be damned if I'll kill us both by trying to make love to you in the pool when we have a house with six empty bedrooms waiting for us." He gave her a smart slap on the rump. "Get moving, Mrs. Fitzhugh. Believe it or not, I have to return to the office this afternoon, but I have no intention of leaving without my . . . lunch."

Shrieking with laughter, she pulled herself out of the pool and started running across the grass toward the house, daring him to catch her. Her long damp hair rose and fell with each step, revealing, then concealing, the symmetry of her figure with graceful provocation. He caught up with her in quick gigantic strides and his hands spanned her waist and pulled her down on the grass on top of him. "To hell with the bedrooms," he decided as his body moved against her and into her. She gasped at the intensity of his emotion and then surrendered herself to the pleasure that awaited her.

How perfect it had been that hot summer day of long ago. The odor of the grass had been unbelievably sweet, and the sun was like a blanket, warming and drying their damp bodies. If only the day had ended then. If only Barbara had not come back and she hadn't learned . . . If only Jamie had not . . . NO! NO! She did not want to think about the rest of it. *Wake up*, her subconscious shouted. *Wake up*!

The morning sun streaming across the bed came to rest on her flushed face. Anxious eyes flew open and quickly surveyed the room, taking in her surroundings. She gave a sigh that could have been regret or relief to find herself in the present, since she was not yet sure just where the real nightmare lay. A quick apprehensive look at the chair by her bed revealed the uniformed figure of a nurse watching her carefully, apparently waiting for her to wake up. "Have you been here all night?" she asked, puzzled, wondering if seeing Jamie had been real or not.

"Yes, Mrs. Fitzhugh"—the nurse smiled down at her—"and it was a bad one for you, wasn't it? But you're much better now. I'll bathe you and then we'll see about breakfast. You'll be hungry now, I'll wager."

Mary looked around the room curiously, seeing it clearly for the first time. It was larger than she remembered hospital rooms as being and too comfortably furnished, painted in soft green with expensive pictures on the wall, and there was a huge bouquet of flowers on a stand by the window.

The nurse followed her glance. "Aren't they lovely? They're from Mrs. Hastings, the mother of the little boy you saved. You're quite the heroine, Mrs. Fitzhugh. The reporters have been waiting to see you since the accident."

"How... how long?"

"Three days," the nurse supplied cheerfully, "and you gave us quite a scare." She filled a basin with warm soapy water as she talked. "We want to make you pretty for the reporters."

Mary shook her head frantically. "No reporters, please."

"Now, don't you get upset, dear. Of course you don't have to see them if you don't feel up to it. But I still want to clean you up and put you into this lovely gown."

Mary stared at the pale ecru satin nightdress the nurse was holding up. "That's not mine."

"Of course it is, dear. Your husband brought it for you, along with all sorts of pretty and sweet-smelling things." As she talked she slipped the rough hospital gown gently off Mary's shoulders and passed first one bandaged hand and then the other. Mary watched, fascinated; her hands looked like two large balloons wrapped in white gauze and reminded her that she was helpless to do anything for herself. Two large tears rolled down her cheeks and she tried awkwardly to brush them away with her arm. "Damn."

Instantly the nurse wiped her face with a wet

washcloth. "Don't worry, dear, it's not as bad as it looks. And I'm here. I'll be your hands for the next few weeks."

"You're a private nurse." It was an accusation, not a question, as Mary took another look at her present surroundings with a horror born of comprehension. "And this is a private suite, isn't it?"

"Of course, dear." Those efficient hands continued their cleansing motions without interruption, washing one exposed limb, toweling it carefully dry, and then proceeding to the other leg, which was heavily wrapped in bandages, so that she had to work carefully around them.

"But I can't afford all this," Mary protested. "My insurance plan at work specifically states a semiprivate room; and certainly no private nurses."

The nurse tutted her objections away. "Nonsense. Mr. Fitzhugh has spoken to me personally. Money is certainly not at issue. Don't worry about a thing. Mr. Fitzhugh has everything well in hand." She slipped the delicate nightdress over Mary's head and pulled it lovingly into place.

"Isn't that pretty on you? And the ones in the drawer are just as beautiful." The nurse's obvious satisfaction at her handiwork, her complacent acceptance of Jamie as being in charge of Mary's life, infuriated her.

"My husband and I don't live—that is, we're separated," Mary said abruptly. "I can't be under obligation to him for any of this."

For the first time the nurse looked disconcerted. "Oh, dear, now. I didn't know." But she instantly resumed her bedside manner. "But you mustn't let it upset you. The important thing is for you to get well and then you can sort out those little details. Right now it's time for your breakfast, and you certainly couldn't handle it without my help, could you?" She hurried out of the room and returned within a few minutes with a tray.

Mary glanced from the tray to her bandaged hands and back again. "Not to worry." The nurse smiled. "I'm going to see that you eat every bite of this."

Mary conceded defeat. She certainly could not do it alone. "What's your name?"

"Jan Wright. I hope you like hot cereal, because you really look like you need building up, Mrs. Fitzhugh."

"Don't call me that." She hesitated, fearing she had been too abrupt. "I don't think of myself as Mrs. Fitzhugh anymore. In fact, I use my maiden name—Mary Karras. That's why I can't understand what my—what Mr. Fitzhugh is doing here. Do you know?"

"It must have been your picture in the *Star*. When no family showed up asking about you after the fire, they ran your picture. Mr. Fitzhugh was here almost as soon as the first edition hit the newsstand; and after talking to your doctor, he hired me to take care of you. Even if you are estranged, you're mighty lucky he turned up when he did, or you would have found yourself in a charity ward."

"Nonsense," Mary said spiritedly. "I have a

job, and health insurance coverage, too." True, her own coverage would provide much more modest accommodations, but she had had four years' practice in living frugally. Much as she would regret leaving this beautiful room, she would have to insist upon being transferred to something more within her price range. She was not about to accept favors from James Calhoun Fitzhugh Jr., after all this time.

She allowed Jan to spoon-feed her while her bandaged hands lay idle in her lap, but between mouthfuls she made it clear that she wanted to see the proper hospital official as soon as possible about a room change.

"This is Sunday," Jan reminded her smoothly. "There won't be anyone you can talk to until tomorrow. By then I'm sure you and Mr. Fitzhugh will have the matter straightened out."

"This does *not* concern Mr. Fitzhugh," Mary insisted. "I don't want him involved in my affairs at all. And if that means that you'll be out of a job, then I'm sorry."

Nurse Wright was not ruffled by a patient's display of temper. She swept the tray off the bed and brought it out to the hall, and when she returned, she fluffed Mary's pillow and wiped her face again with a moist cloth. "Would you like me to make up your face a bit? Perhaps a bit of blusher to put some color in your cheeks and some lip gloss to keep your lips from drying out."

"Don't fuss over me," Mary snapped. "I can't afford you and I have no intention of getting used to your services."

Jan turned her attention to rearranging the flowers. "Well, we'll work out the cost later, shall we? Your hands will be wrapped in bandages for at least two or three weeks, and until then you are going to need help."

Mary took a deep breath. She was really too tired to think out all the details clearly and her hands were starting to throb again. "When I go home, I'm sure my neighbor will help out, if she's anywhere near as grateful as you said she was about her little boy."

The nurse managed a sympathetic smile. "I thought you realized that you won't be able to return to your apartment. The entire building was pretty well destroyed."

Mary tried not to show how this information shocked her, but in spite of her good intentions, tears welled in her eyes. "Everything I owned—everything Stash owned—was in that apartment. What will I do?"

Instantly the matronly nurse was at her side with a tissue, dabbing at the tears. "There, there, Mrs. Fitzhugh. You'll make yourself worse with those tears. Try not to dwell on what happened. Be grateful that you escaped with your life. Everything else will fall into place. Not to worry. I'll take care of you as long as you need me. Now, close your eyes and sleep awhile more."

Mary sniffed and brought her shattered emotions under control. The nurse was right. It was foolish to worry about anything until she was well enough to handle it. The important thing was to get well as fast as she could. "My hands are starting to be quite painful," she said, determined to concentrate on her physical problems, rather than her emotional ones. "Do you think I might have something for the pain?"

"Ah, dear, it's a mite too early yet. The doctor wants us to start spacing the medication a little farther apart. We don't want you to get too dependent on it, do we? Just try to sleep, and in another hour I can give you something."

Obediently Mary closed her eyes. She was tired, and the pulses in the palms of her hands were throbbing strongly now, but the pain was nothing compared to what she had endured these past years—a pain that had, at last, started to abate, until she had seen Jamie again. *Oh, Mrs. Wright*, she thought, *you would be surprised at the amount of pain I can bear.*

It wasn't the pain that frightened her, it was the helplessness. In the past, no matter how badly things had gone for her, she had always been able to depend upon her own youthful strength and resiliency to carry her through. Now, finding herself totally dependent on others, she was frightened for the first time.

She needed someone, and the only person in the world she could depend upon was her half-brother, Stan Templeton; and he was over 3,000 miles and an ocean away, while Jamie, from whom she had fled four years ago, was here, threatening to destroy her life again. She felt instinctively that the past was about to come crashing down around her, and she was helpless to do anything about it.

Chapter Two

The rest of that day passed in a flurry of hospital routine intermingled with visitors. The doctor came and examined her bandages and told her she was a brave and lucky lady. More flowers were delivered; these from the office where Mary was a bookkeeper. Her boss, Mr. Evans, surprised her with a personal visit and set her mind at rest by promising that her job would be waiting for her. He told her also that she was courageous and added shyly that he was proud to know her.

Mr. Evans was a sweet middle-aged widower. He had asked Mary out socially on numerous occasions, and even though she had firmly refused him each time, there had never been any awkwardness between them. He still counted himself lucky to have such an efficient worker and had resigned himself to having nothing more than her polite friendship. He was a nice man, and Mary was touched when he had added his own modest flowers to the formal arrangement sent by the office.

Nancy Hastings stopped in and hugged Mary

and cried and promised never, ever again to leave her son alone even for a moment. She brought Mary's purse, which was all she had managed to salvage from the smoke-filled ruins of their apartment building, and told Mary she could live with her when she was released from the hospital. Of course, Nancy had not yet found a place to live and was staying with friends, but she assured Mary that wherever she lived, Mary would always be welcome.

Considering that they had never had more than a nodding acquaintance before the fire, Mary was both embarrassed and skeptical of her demonstrations of emotion and could only lie there helplessly as Nancy babbled on and on. Finally Jan, noticing her patient's weariness, suggested that perhaps it would be best if Mrs. Hastings planned their future at a later date.

The pain in her hands and leg was making itself felt again, but Mary did not mention it. She knew that when it was time for more medication, Jan would see to it. She closed her eyes wearily against the pain and tried to rest while Jan sat in the chair by the bed, watching soap operas on the TV. Eventually the sound of the slick voices droning on in the despair that made them so popular put Mary to sleep.

When she woke again, there were more flowers in the room and a stack of get-well cards, all of them from strangers. She was a real celebrity, Jan told her proudly and suggested that perhaps she should see those reporters after all, since heroines had a responsibility to their public. Mary shuddered at the thought and lay back and listened as Jan read the cards aloud to her. She thought it silly that perfect strangers should be writing to her, but it was rather a pleasant sensation to receive mail. In the past four years, other than her utility bills, she had perhaps received a total of six postcards from Stash, sent from the various exotic capitals of the world he happened to be working in at the time.

Stash. It was her childhood name for him, and when she referred to him aloud, she tried to remember to call him Stan, or John, which he preferred; but now, in her helplessness, the little girl in her could think of him only as Stash, the big brother she had always turned to for help. Thinking of him now reminded Mary that she would have to write to him and tell him that his lovely apartment was destroyed along with all his prize possessions. How he would hate that.

Stash was an engineer whose job kept him traveling most of the time, and his apartment was the anchor he kept in civilization—the place where he could return and be surrounded by the beautiful objects he was continually collecting, but which he could not take with him as he moved from assignment to assignment.

When Mary had come running to him for help that terrible day, it had been just blind luck that he was in the country at all, but he had taken her in without hesitation. When it was time for him to leave on another overseas assignment, they had decided that she would stay on, taking care of the apartment and the valuable objects that he had collected. He continued to pay the rent and was quick to make Mary feel that her services as curator of his own private museum-apartment adequately covered her share of the rent. This small financial help on his part had been a godsend for Mary, for then her small bookkeeper's salary was just enough to make ends meet.

On those semiannual vacation visits when her half-brother returned to the apartment, it was crowded, but both were so happy with the arrangement that they concentrated on enjoying each other's company rather than complaining because one or the other of them had to sleep on the sofa of the one-bedroom apartment. Each of his trips home was accompanied by another artifact to be admired and suitably positioned. Such beautiful, valuable things, each with a special memory for Stash, and now they were gone.

Mary gave a sigh that caused Jan to break off her reading of the cards, and asked her nurse to write a letter for her. Then, as quickly and as simply as she could, she dictated a letter to Stash, telling him that his possessions had been destroyed in a fire that gutted their apartment building and that his insurance company would be notified. She felt compelled to say that she had hurt her hands slightly, to explain the strange handwriting, but that she was otherwise fine and would send him her new address as soon as she had one. She apologized profusely for letting him down and closed with much love.

Disregarding the intensely disapproving look that crossed Jan's face as she wrote the dictated

words, Mary had her address an envelope to Mr.
S. John Templeton, which was the name Stash
was known by at work, and watched carefully to
make sure that she wrote it correctly and affixed
enough postage to it.

"Were there any other letters you wanted me
to write, Mrs. Fitzhugh?"

"Karras," Mary corrected. "I told you, I use
my maiden name—Mary Karras. But, please call
me Mary." She indicated the letter. "When you
bring it down to the main desk to mail it, be sure
to give them my correct name. And no, there are
no other letters." She could have added, but did
not, that she did not know another soul in the
world who would want to hear from her, who
would even care if she were alive or dead, she
thought with painful honesty as she closed her
eyes.

That was why she was so surprised when she
awoke again to find Jamie—James Calhoun Fitzhugh Jr.—sitting at her bedside, waiting for her to
wake up. Almost as a reflex action she clamped
her eyes shut and pretended to be asleep, hoping
that he had not noticed her movement, hoping
that he would go away.

Jamie had never been a man to be put off. "I
know you're awake, Mary, and pretending you're
not is just wasting both our time." His voice was
pleasant enough to fool Jan, but Mary was not
misled. He had called her Mary, and that was not
his name for her.

Long ago, when she had confided to him that
her parents called her Manya as a child, he had

adopted that name as his own special address for her. To Fitz, Jamie's father, and their friends she remained Mary, because it had such a proper Scottish lilt to it, did Mary Fitzhugh. And, of course, his father's housekeeper, Barbara, had followed Fitz's lead. Manya Fitzhugh would never do for Fitz. He considered it discordant, like opposite worlds colliding, and Jamie had been delighted at his father's attitude, since it meant that only he used that pet name for her.

Beneath closed lids she tried to think of herself as Manya Fitzhugh and cringed. The words together rasped in her mind like a fingernail on a blackboard. She never wanted to be called Manya or Fitzhugh again. Plain Mary Karras suited her just fine.

"There are things we have to discuss," he insisted, forcing himself into the private darkness of her thoughts.

"I'll just go and mail her letter," Jan said, rising to assure them of privacy. Jamie's steel-gray eyes took in the name on the envelope and his lips tightened almost into a snarl.

"Not too ill to write to the boyfriend, I see. Well, you can damn well open your eyes and talk to me."

Mary knew better than to deny that tone of voice. Her eyes opened, and a heavy weight settled on her chest, taking her breath away as she looked at him. His sandy hair was as curly and thick as she remembered it, cut in a no-nonsense style that tried unsuccessfully to keep it in line. The almost opaque clarity of his eyes was devoid of emotion as he stared down at her, but his long straight nose flared slightly, betraying that he was not as calm as he appeared to be. Only the wide grin she knew so well was absent, and the sensual lower lip was drawn into a tight, thin slash.

"How could you?" he accused without preamble. He had waited too long to ask this question to be put off any longer. "How could you leave me and Cal without a word of explanation, to live with another man? Were you having an affair with him all the time I thought you were mine alone? When I held you in my arms and made love to you, were you comparing me with him and finding me lacking?" The note of anguish in his voice was quickly conquered and changed to indifference. "Not that I give a damn any longer," he hastened to add, "but a man gets curious about such things."

Mary caught her breath at his attack. So that was how he was going to play it. She was to be the villain in the piece, was she? What nonsense was he spouting about another man? He knew as well as she did that Stan Templeton was her half-brother. He was obviously taking an innocent situation and putting the worst possible interpretation on it to discredit her in an attempt to whitewash himself in the eyes of their friends.

Well, he could continue to do so for all she cared. She had no need to defend herself at this late stage of the game. The truth was so much worse that she would willingly settle for his version if only it would allow the matter to drop so that she would not have to think about what really happened.

In spite of herself, she found she was staring at him, drinking in every detail of his appearance. Why couldn't she just hate him and be done with it? For four years she had managed to survive by feeding on her hatred, and now, just seeing him again, it faded away to nothing, leaving her defenseless. In the far recesses of her mind she had always known it would be so, and that was why she had so carefully avoided seeing him. If he wanted, she knew he could make her forgive him anything just for another chance to be in his arms.

"I hate you," she said adamantly, as though by saying the words aloud she could resurrect her armor.

"And what about Cal?" he accused. "Do you hate him, too? Is that why you left him?"

In spite of her resolve not to let him hurt her, she flinched, and tears welled in her eyes, tears that she commanded herself not to shed. "I would have taken him with me, if I could." Her words were barely a whisper.

"What's the matter, didn't your boyfriend want him? Or would three have been a crowd in that sordid one-bedroom love nest in Grandview?"

"You knew where I was?" she gasped.

"From the second week."

"But you never tried to get in touch with me."

He disposed of her with a glance. "Your boyfriend might want another man's leavings, but I didn't."

That hit a nerve. "Neither did I," she snapped back.

"What the hell is that supposed to mean?"

Mary retreated. She would not be trapped into talking to him about it. She swallowed and shrugged the question aside without answering. "I suppose you're here to ask about a divorce."

He gave an unpleasant laugh. "Surely you recall that the Fitzhughs do *not* divorce. Didn't Fitz and my mother impress that upon you?"

"I thought you might have learned something from their mistakes," she jeered and knew a moment of vindictive pleasure when she saw his lips tighten.

She had taken an unfair shot and she knew it. His parents had lived estranged for twenty years without having divorced. One day his mother had simply walked out on Fitz, taking her daughter, Rebecca, with her and leaving her older seventeen-year-old son behind. Once, in a moment of vulnerability, Jamie had confided to Mary how much that rejection had hurt him.

Years later he and his mother had made up, and after his marriage to Mary, they had visited Helene Fitzhugh several times at her lavish oceanfront condominium in Cocoa Beach. The two women had become friends, but Jamie and his mother remained friendly strangers.

Mary had always felt that Fitz would take his wife back in a second, if she were willing. After each visit with Helene, they could expect to be cross-examined in detail by Fitz on everything his wife had said and done. It was his one vulnerable area, and it always hurt Mary to admit to him that Helene never spoke his name or allowed it to be brought into a conversation. Invariably his features would darken and he would once again become the ruthless, autocratic head of Fitzhugh Industries.

"Why doesn't she divorce him if she hates him so?" Mary had asked Jamie after one of their trips to Florida to see his mother. Jamie had replied, "Because Fitz won't allow it. We're Catholic and politically prominent; therefore, the Fitzhughs do not divorce." And then Jamie had pulled her tightly into his arms and bent his head to rest against her forehead.

"We're so lucky, Manya. Those two loved each other once, but somewhere along the way they lost it. Mom won't even talk about it, but it's obvious that Fitz still loves her even after all these years."

If Fitz did love his wife, Mary thought he had a strange way of showing it. He had had numerous mistresses over the years. Some of them had made no pretense of their role in Fitz's life, while others had discreetly cloaked their relationship behind such euphemisms as business associate, secretary, or housekeeper.

Mary's eyes narrowed as this last category led her mind back to the present and into channels she did not want to dwell upon. "Is Barbara still your father's housekeeper?" The words were out before she could stop them, but he did not notice how distressed she was to have actually spoken her thoughts aloud.

"As a matter of fact, she is. The house would fall apart without her. And, of course, her daughter is company for Cal. We live there now, you know."

She thought her chest would explode with the pain. "Her...her daughter?"

He seemed surprised she did not know. "Yes, it seems Barb was secretly married about five years ago. It was a mistake, and she's since been divorced, but she has a beautiful daughter. She was born about seven months after you—" He left the sentence unfinished. "Well, I'm sure that wouldn't interest you in any way."

She fought to catch her breath. The color drained from her face so rapidly that her lips turned blue and her teeth chattered despite her efforts to still them. Her acute physical distress was apparent even to Jamie's unfriendly appraisal.

"What's wrong?" he asked in alarm, and when she stared at him, unable to say a word or catch her breath, he ran into the hallway and literally picked a nurse up from her station and brought her back with him into the room. Jan, who was returning from her errand, followed close behind, and the two nurses shooed him out of the room and turned their attentions to their patient.

"Are you in pain, Mary?" Jan inquired anxiously. "Is that what's wrong?"

At Jan's words, Mary started to pound her bandaged hands frantically against the bed, impervious to the pain that resulted. The tears she had been holding back flooded over, and she began to moan, helpless to stop herself as her voice pitched upward to an anguished scream. Only the merciful administration of a sedative by the hall nurse brought her hysteria to a halt.

It was hours later before she came to. "I don't want to ever see him again," she said dully. Jan looked anxious, but Mary was calm now and determined not to lose control again. "I won't be needing any more injections, either. I guess I just had a delayed reaction to the shock of the accident." Her voice dared Jan to contradict her, but Jan merely nodded, and Mary let the matter drop. She had been a fool to go to pieces, but it would not happen again. It was the first time in four years she had allowed herself the luxury of self-pity, and it would be a long time before she did so again.

It was not as though this were the first blow fate had dealt her. Her mother had died when she was very young, and her father had been left a bitter, unloving man who thought material things could substitute for affection in a young girl's life. It had been up to her older half-brother, Stash, to supply what little affection she had known as a child; but as a stepson, he shared even less of her father's regard than she did, and when he left for college on a scholarship, Mary knew that he would never return home to live again.

She had just turned seventeen when her father died, leaving her their small house and enough money to finish business school, if she were very frugal. Stash had been too far away even to return for the funeral, and she felt guilty because she did not miss either of them. She had been alone for so long, she did not even realize how empty her life was until she met Jamie.

No. She wouldn't think about that. Her life had *not* been empty. It had been calm, predictable, and untroubled. Just as it was after she left Jamie. Just as it would be again.

"Pardon me," Jan broke through her concentration, "but there's a Mr. Fitzhugh to see you." She saw Mary stiffen and she continued hurriedly, "Not *him*. Another older, more"—she waved her hands, at a loss for the right words—"more blustery, and . . . and bossy, and he insists on seeing you. I'm sorry, Mary, but he just won't go away."

Mary took a deep, resigned breath. Fitz was here. She could almost sympathize with Jan's discomfort. Meeting Fitz for the first time was like being mowed down by a bulldozer. Poor Jan was probably thinking that if Jamie could upset her patient to the point of hysteria, Fitz would eat her alive. She couldn't know that Fitz was the one Fitzhugh male who did not have the power to hurt her. Mary flashed her a reassuring smile. "It's all right, Jan. Tell him to come in and then take a break. This Mr. Fitzhugh and I have always understood one another."

Surprised and a little confused at Mary's calm acceptance of this formidable visitor, Jan wavered uncertainly for a moment before moving with some reluctance to carry out her instructions. "I'll be right outside the door," she reassured Mary, "so call out if you need me."

A moment later Fitz strode into the room, dominating it. As usual, he entered with an air that made Mary think that trumpets should blare forth announcing his presence; but she refused to be impressed.

Looking at him, she saw a preview of what Jamie would look like in another twenty-five years. He was as tall as his son, but about fifty pounds heavier, and his sandy hair had diminished to a curly gray fringe, but his gray eyes were every bit as sharp and piercing as Jamie's.

"Well, Mary, it's been a long time," he boomed with disarming cheerfulness as he sank into the chair by her bed. The differences between him and Jamie were also obvious to her. Jamie's strength was quiet, understated, his emotions always carefully hidden beneath a sophisticated veneer. Fitz was flamboyant, abrasive, domineering. Both could be ruthless, but Fitz was prouder of this trait and flaunted it. He was quick to seize any initiative that would put the other person at a disadvantage, but Mary was not intimidated by him.

"Have you missed me, Fitz?" she jibed.

"Not for a minute." His gray eyes bored into hers. "You were never the right wife for Jamie, and I told him so before he insisted on marrying you. I told you so, too, at the time, if you remember."

Oh, yes, she remembered. He had not only told her so, but he had tried to buy her off, and when that had not worked, he had threatened to disinherit his son; when that had not worked, he had sent Jamie out of the country on company business. His fury, when he learned that they had used Jamie's supposed exile to Greece for a honeymoon, had been uncontained. For Mary and Jamie the month of incredible joy that they had known in Greece had made facing Fitz on their return a small enough price to pay, and surprisingly enough, because "the Fitzhughs did not divorce," he had finally accepted their marriage. When Cal was born, nine months later, he had been beside himself with family pride.

As though reading her thoughts, he said, "The only good thing that came out of that marriage was Cal. Jamie's done a damn fine job of raising him," he added with typical bluntness.

Mary did not even flinch. One always knew where one stood with Fitz, and now that she was not part of his grand family plan, she really did not care what he thought.

"Why are you here, Fitz?" She could be blunt, too. "I'm sure you're not concerned about my health."

"Come on now, Mary," he chided, "that's not fair. I was against your marriage, sure, but after it was done, I always treated you right, didn't I? You know my feelings on the sanctity of marriage."

"Yes, both you and Helene have mentioned it," she said with unveiled sarcasm and was instantly ashamed when she saw the quick flicker of pain in his eyes before he carefully erased it. Helene, it seemed, was still his Achilles' heel.

"The trouble with you is that you're too much like Helene," he attacked. "Both of you are too weak to be Fitzhugh women. At the first sign of trouble, you collapse like insipid Victorian virgins. I don't know what caused the rift between you and Jamie, but I do know a stronger woman could have coped."

"Well, that's all water under the dam, isn't it, Fitz?" She managed to keep her voice level. "I really don't care to discuss what might have been with you."

"Then let's talk about what will be," he demanded harshly, leaning toward her prone figure on the bed. "I don't suppose Jamie got a chance to tell you yesterday that our party has selected him to run for Congress in November."

"How nice for him, but it hardly concerns me, does it?"

"It damn well does concern you now that you've made a public spectacle of yourself with this fire episode. Little lady, you are this close to ruining everything we've worked for these past few years." He held his thumb and forefinger close to her face in a menacing gesture.

Mary gave him a level look until he backed slightly away from her, but his eyes continued to hold hers.

"Why should my being in that fire make any difference to Jamie's political plans?" She was curious in spite of herself.

He gave a snort of disgust. "Don't you know anything about politics? A wife is a candidate's greatest asset. In Jamie's case I had to do some pretty fancy footwork to get the Party to accept the fact that he had a quiet, dignified separation; and they went along with me because, after all, he was a devoted father with custody of the boy and he was obviously the injured party."

Mary accepted that bit of information with a slightly raised eyebrow, but Fitz ignored it. "But you couldn't stay out of the picture, could you? You had to pull some damn-fool stunt to save a kid and get your picture in all the papers. Now everyone is asking why their prospective candidate and his heroine of a wife aren't together. Candidates *do not* get separated from wives that are heroines," he sneered, "it makes bad copy."

"Too bad," she observed without sympathy. "I guess Jamie will just have to settle for being the most expensive corporate lawyer in the state."

"You are *not* going to louse this up for him!" A dull, angry flush flooded his face. "I'll make you wish you had never been born, if you do."

Mary shrugged. "Since I already wish that quite often, that's not much of a threat. Besides, there's not much I can do about it, is there? Jamie and I *are* separated, and I guess I am a heroine of sorts to the newspapers. Of course, if I had known at the time how much it meant to Jamie's career, I suppose I could have let the boy die for old times' sake."

"Don't be flip with me," he growled. "I'm going to see that Jamie comes out of this smelling like a rose, and you're going to help me, do you understand?"

"Yes and no." She was rather enjoying his discomfort. It wasn't often that Fitz was in a situation where he wasn't in total control. "That is, yes, I understand what you are saying; but no, I am not going to help you. There's nothing I can do to change the situation, and if there were,'' she said frankly, "I wouldn't do it. I'm done with the Fitzhughs.''

"Even Cal?'' He played his trump card. "He's grown quite a bit since you last saw him. He's only seven, but sprouting like a weed and smart as a whip. Would you like to see a picture of him?''

That wasn't fair. He was hitting below the belt and he knew it. It was so long since she had last held that loving towheaded baby in her arms. That last time she had squeezed him to her so tightly before leaving the house that he had cried. In her mind's eye she could see him still, crying, his arms outstretched, asking her to pick him up and comfort him. Instead she had set him in his crib and called to the housekeeper to sit with him until Jamie came home. He had been a chubby baby of three then. What did he look like at seven?

She bit her lip. "I don't want to see the picture," she blurted. "All children look the same.''

He wasn't fooled. Fumbling in his wallet, he withdrew a small snapshot that he thrust under her nose. "He's a good-looking kid, isn't he?''

She closed her eyes and turned her face away. She had been wrong. Fitz did have the power to hurt her, after all. "Go away.''

"Just look at your son," he insisted.

"If you don't go away, I'll scream," she said in desperation, "and I'll keep screaming until they take you out of here.''

He gave an ugly laugh. "You've got that all wrong, honey. After the fit you threw yesterday, if you start screaming now, the men in the white suits will put you in a rubber room. Go ahead," he taunted, "maybe that would solve all our problems. A candidate with a wife in the looney bin should get a lot of sympathy votes."

"What do you want of me, Fitz?" The words were wrung from her.

"Open your eyes and look at your son," he coaxed.

Mary knew he would not budge from her room until she did as he asked, and besides, she desperately wanted to see what Cal—what her son—looked like. Her thick blond lashes lifted, revealing beaten blue eyes that reproached him for making her do this, and then they fixed hungrily on the picture he was holding up.

Such a handsome boy. The chubby baby fat she remembered had been replaced by a scrawny, growing-boy body. The sandy Fitzhugh hair curled shaggily on his collar, with a fringe of would-be bangs brushed to one side of his high forehead. The eyes were wide-spaced, Fitzhugh gray, but eager, inquiring, innocent as no other Fitzhugh she knew, and his smile proudly displayed two missing front teeth. He was not the baby she had left behind, and yet, she felt instinctively that if she had passed him on the street, she would have known him. He looked like the pictures she had seen of Jamie at that age; in fact, everything about him said Fitzhugh. There was nothing of her in him at all, she thought bitterly; any woman could have been his mother.

Mary turned her face away, but not before the

image had been carefully stored in her memory. "Well, I've seen it." She forced a briskness to her voice. "Now what?"

"Mary, Mary," he rebuked, "don't try to con a con man. You don't have to pretend with me. I'm here to help you."

She did not bother to answer that.

"I'm giving you a chance to start over—to make a home for your husband and your son. Jamie wants to be a family again."

"Jamie hates me," she reminded him and added quickly, "and I hate him."

He raised his hands in a pacifying gesture. "Whatever happened between the two of you is over four years old. Jamie is willing to forgive and forget if you are. For Cal's sake."

"For the voters' sake, don't you mean," she exploded. "The two of you would do or say anything to get him elected. Well, you're wasting your time. Nothing could persuade me to live with Jamie again."

"I'm not talking about sharing his bed," Fitz said with characteristic bluntness, "just his house. It's a big house," he coaxed. "You wouldn't have to see much of each other. He'd be campaigning most of the time, and you would have the house—and Cal—to yourself. You'd like that, wouldn't you?"

"No."

"The election is only six months away," he continued smoothly, ignoring her interruption. "After that, he would be living in the Capitol for over half the year. You could stay on in the Kansas City house with Cal, or perhaps by then we could even arrange another discreet separation with shared custody of Cal.''

''No.''

The dull red flush spread over his face again, warning her that he was out of patience. ''Damn it, Mary, that was the good news. That was Jamie's offer because he didn't want to hurt you or Cal. But if you don't go for it, then we'll do things my way, and believe me, you'll like that a lot less!''

''And what is your way?'' She was only mildly curious. There was nothing he could propose that would make her return to Jamie. And as for Cal—she had been out of his life a long time now, and it would be less disturbing for him if she stayed that way.

''My way,'' Fitz continued with quiet menace, ''is a quick, very dirty, very ugly divorce. Dragging you into court, proving your infidelity, showing the world you're an unfit mother and that Jamie was a saint to put up with you as long as he did for the child's sake. By the time I get through with you, you'll be the most notorious woman in the state of Missouri. It's the way I wanted to handle it from the beginning. You won't be much of a heroine after I've proved to the world that you're nothing but a tramp! And I promise you that the sympathy and support that Jamie will get from the media will guarantee him the election. It will be tough on Cal, of course, to have his mother's name dragged through the gutter, but he'll get over it.''

The color drained from her face. "You're bluffing. Jamie wouldn't let you put Cal through that."

"Ha!" he barked, "Jamie won't be able to stop me. Once I start this smear campaign, it will go forward on its own momentum. I'd do anything to get him elected to Congress, even go against his wishes if I felt it would be in his best interest."

Mary knew he was telling the truth, but what he didn't know was that she could make such a smear boomerang on Jamie. She tried to tell him so. "There are things I could say that would do Jamie a lot of harm."

"It needn't come to that, if you're smart." He retreated just the littlest bit. "We can still do the loving family bit for the voters. But if we don't, if we end up airing our dirty linen in public, then I guarantee we will come out on top. The loser will be Cal. If you don't care about what the publicity does to him, then I warn you, I don't either."

"I thought you loved Cal," she flung out bitterly.

"I'm crazy about the kid, and you know it," he countered, "but he's a Fitzhugh; he'll survive. In fact, if I put it to him that it was necessary to do that to get his father elected to Congress, he'd testify against you himself. After all, he doesn't owe you a thing."

"It's not me I'm concerned about. Believe me, Fitz, a scandal won't hurt me. It could only hurt Jamie and Cal...and you," she added desperately. "I don't expect you to believe me, but it's true."

He looked at her thoughtfully. "Maybe you do

know something I don't, but I'm willing to take that chance. I'll gamble Cal's piece of mind, his love for his father, his ability to cope with the taunts of his friends. Will you?"

When she did not answer, he rose. "Well, that's it, then. I've come prepared to release the whole sordid story to the press. There are still a lot of reporters milling about in the halls, hoping to interview their 'heroine'. I think I can give them a story that will garner even bigger headlines. I even have a press release prepared that should get their undivided attention." He reached into his jacket pocket and pulled out a sheaf of papers that he glanced through. "So long, Mary. See you in court." He walked to the door.

She gasped. He was really going to do it—sacrifice his grandson's piece of mind for political advantage. Did he really think that the little boy of those wide innocent eyes could come through such a scandal unscathed?

If she told the truth—that she had been living with her brother, not a lover—she would have to explain why she really left Jamie and ruin Cal's image of his father. If she said nothing and allowed them to believe that Stash was her lover, then he would hate her as Jamie did. Perhaps he hated her already anyway.

If it weren't for Cal, she would let Fitz do his worst. What revenge it would be on the both of them when such a smear campaign backfired. But there was Cal to consider. He would be crushed by the knowledge that the one remaining parent he had come to depend upon had feet of clay. He didn't deserve to have his dreams crushed.

Damn the Fitzhughs for wanting to have their own way regardless of who was hurt. Well, she wasn't Fitzhugh enough for that. She looked at Fitz's retreating back and knew he would not come back unless she agreed to his terms.

"Fitz," she whispered frantically. He stopped and turned back to look at her, a half smile playing on his lips.

"Wait," she sobbed, "I've—I've changed my mind."

Chapter Three

A week later Mary was wheeled out of the hospital and into the chauffeur-driven limousine that was waiting in the no-parking zone. Jan settled her carefully into the backseat and then climbed in beside her. Jamie waited until the two women were settled in and then he slid in smoothly to sit on Mary's other side. A mob of reporters and cameramen followed them with curious eyes, hurling questions and popping flashbulbs at them constantly.

Mary shrank from their bold stares and bolder questions, and Jamie flung an arm protectively around her shoulders as he flashed a disarming smile at the reporters. "Take it easy, guys. Mrs. Fitzhugh isn't used to your wild ways, so give her a break. I promise she'll give you an in-depth interview as soon as the doctor gives his okay."

As if on cue, the engine of the powerful car roared to a start and pulled away from the curb, but not before Mary, with a gentle assist from Jamie, waved one bandaged hand in a timid farewell to the press. Flashbulbs exploded in delighted approval of the gesture as they zoomed away.

As soon as they were out of sight Jamie's arm fell stiffly to his side and he shifted his position slightly so that his body no longer touched hers. Reaching into his briefcase, he withdrew some mimeographed material and proceeded to give his work his entire concentration.

Mary suppressed a sigh and tried to interest herself in the scenery they were passing. His actions were merely a repeat of the many scenes that had passed between them since she had succumbed to Fitz's blackmail. Immediately after her capitulation, Fitz had taken his triumphant departure, and later that afternoon, Jamie, himself, had appeared to finalize the details of the arrangement with her.

Their first order of business was to agree upon the story they would release to the press. Jamie had definite ideas as to what that story should be; their four-year separation was to be explained as a misunderstanding on his part and amnesia on hers. He then proceeded to outline the details to her in his usual autocratic manner.

"My mother was visiting New York about the time you disappeared. We'll say we had a quarrel and you decided to join her there for a few days to think things over. However, she was not in her hotel room when you arrived, so you left word for her at the desk and went for a walk in the park. You never returned.

"Naturally, she was frantic and contacted me. I flew to New York and engaged a team of detectives to search for you. To no avail. There was no trace of you in the hospitals, the jails, or the morgue—in short, no sign of foul play. I could only assume that you had deliberately disappeared because of the silly quarrel we had had before you left.

"The detectives continued to search for you, but I returned to Kansas City—to our son," he added with malicious emphasis, "and tried to pick up the broken pieces of our life. It was obvious to everyone that my wife had deserted me, and they were all very sympathetic. Women were especially sympathetic," he informed her silkily.

Mary ignored the jibe. "But now I've returned and I'm an obvious embarrassment to you; forcing you to reconcile the previous impression you gave your friends and the press of a callous, unfeeling wife and mother with their 'heroine of the hour,' who risked her life to save a child. How do you intend to do that?" she challenged.

"That's where the amnesia comes in," he shot back, obviously having given the matter some prior thought. "While you were walking in the park, you were mugged; hit over the head, robbed, and left unconscious. When you came to, your memory was a shambles; like a jigsaw puzzle with most of the pieces missing. Most, but not all," he emphasized.

"Your purse was gone and with it your identification. Luckily, most of your money was stuffed into a French purse in your jacket pocket, so you weren't penniless. However, you were confused and had no idea of what you were doing in New

York. As you wandered around the city things came back to you—your old hometown, your maiden name, the death of your father. You bought a newspaper and discovered you had lost the last four years of your life. In effect, you had forgotten me and Cal.''

''How convenient for your story.'' She could not resist the taunt.

He gave her a measured look. ''Not at all. The medical experts I've consulted have told me that selective amnesia is quite common. The patient retreats from a present trauma to a past traumatic period—your father's death in this case.'' At her unbelieving stare he continued smoothly. ''Naturally, they will say the same thing to the press when questioned.''

Naturally. He would insist on the testimony of experts to substantiate his story. She shrugged her shoulders dismissively and waited for him to continue.

''When it became obvious to you that you could not remember anything beyond your father's death, you bought a bus ticket to the town you remembered—Grandview, Missouri—and decided to return there and try to discover your identity.''

''But of course I was unsuccessful,'' she concluded wearily.

''Of course,'' he agreed. ''You hadn't lived in Grandview in years and you had no family left there at all. Nobody remembered you. But you decided it was as good a place as any to stay until the rest of your memory returned. Meanwhile, I continued to search for you in New York City, the last place you had been seen, unaware that you were only twenty-five miles away from our home in Mission Hills. Of course, neither of us was to know this until the fire reunited us.''

Up to this point he had been filling in the details in a matter-of-fact, almost bored manner. Now, however, he fixed a malevolent look on her pale features, as if to emphasize the importance of his next remarks. ''Luckily for our story, your boyfriend was not living with you at the time, so we won't have to mention him at all. Somehow I think any mention of your lover would sully the story we've concocted of an innocent and confused amnesia victim. As far as the rest of the world is concerned, you were living alone, is that understood?''

She realized that now was the time to tell him that Stash was her half-brother, not her lover, but she refused to give him the satisfaction. Let him suffer as she had suffered. As he methodically tied together the loose ends of the story, he hardly looked at her, but he weaved the deceptive tale so skillfully that she was more convinced than ever that it was a talent he had perfected during the years of their marriage. She refused to add a word to the lies that came so easily to his lips, and he had to be content to interpret her silence as assent in all the proper places.

When he had finished talking and she still had nothing to say, he quirked his lips derisively. ''The press will eat the story up. It has all the corny elements of melodrama that they thrive on.''

His voice was mocking, trying to pierce her stoic reserve, but behind his glib words he could not help wishing that the story he had strung together were really the truth. If only she had been an innocent victim of amnesia. The long agony of their separation would have been worth it, if in the end his foolish illusions about her had remained intact.

But Mary wasn't innocent. No use to torture himself thinking of what might have been. The fact remained, she had left him for another man's bed. Why did it still hurt just to look at her? Surely the defenses he had managed to build up over the past four years against just such a moment should be protection enough.

His eyes narrowed as he surveyed her wan face and pitifully thin body with a critical eye. Even her once-magnificent hair was limp and drab against the stark white hospital pillow. There was nothing there now to tempt a man to make a fool of himself. So why did he avoid looking into her eyes where traces of banked blue fire still blazed accusingly at him? If he did not keep his guard up, they would have him believing that somehow this whole sorry mess was his fault. Once those eyes had read the secrets of his soul, but he would not give them that opportunity again.

Get off my back, he growled silently, and then, to punish her for disturbing his thoughts so insidiously, he insisted on going over the whole sorry story aloud one more time.

Mary stirred restlessly, but only once did she try to assert herself, and that was when he spoke of their living in Fitz's huge mansion, where he and Cal had been staying since she left. Her eyes narrowed speculatively at the cozy picture this conjured up of Fitz and Jamie and Cal all living under the same roof with Barbara, who was apparently still Fitz's housekeeper, and, of course, Barbara's daughter. The fact that there was also a full staff of servants to complete the picture did nothing to distract from the intimacy of the situation that Mary envisioned with bitterness. . . . Just one big happy family.

"If I have to live in the same house with—" She caught herself just in time. "If I have to live in Fitz's house, the deal is off," she said with a venom that made Jamie look up quickly.

"Well, where the hell did you expect me to take you?" Jamie countered derisively. "I closed up our Mission Hills house when you walked out on me."

She hesitated, not knowing exactly what she did want. She did not want to live in their old house either, with all the memories she had tried so hard to put out of her mind, but neither did she want to share a house with Jamie and Barbara. In the end she agreed to live in Fitz's house for a few weeks, and he promised to consider reopening their old house and hiring new staff.

Barbara and her child would have to be faced eventually, but with Jan's help, Mary was determined to avoid them as much as possible. She would have her meals in her room and would not leave the wing of the house assigned to her.

At the same time Jamie made it quite clear that

while he would be occupying the same wing of the house with her, they would be having little or no contact with each other except for rare public appearances. He made no secret of the fact that this temporary arrangement was as distasteful to him as it was to her.

"Then why are you forcing me into this position?" Mary asked with a bitterness she could not conceal.

Jamie's gray eyes were cold with loathing as he looked at her. "I don't expect you to understand," he told her, "but I have a lot of ideas on how to improve things in this country, and in order to put my ideas into practice, I have to get elected to office. I'm not going to allow the fact that I have an unfaithful wife to keep me from doing the work I'm best at. If I have to be a happily married man to gain the necessary votes, then that's exactly what I intend to be. And I warn you, lady, you will not be running out on me this time unless I say you can leave. Is that understood?"

Mary shrugged her shoulders, pretending an indifference she did not feel at the scorn in his voice. It must be obvious, even to him, that she would not be going anywhere with one leg and both hands immobilized.

His position painfully clear, they settled into a routine wherein he came to the hospital each day to see her—and to be seen doing so by the reporters camped outside her rooms, waiting for human interest items. He would stay exactly one hour, during which time he read the newspaper or worked on the files in his briefcase. At the end of that time he would rise abruptly and leave without a word.

At first she had hoped that he would bring Cal with him, but Jamie insisted that the reporters would disturb and frighten the boy, and they had agreed that it would be best to postpone her first meeting with him until she left the hospital. At least, that was what Jamie had decided, and Mary apparently had no option but to go along with his plans.

"Are you all right, Mary?" Jan's calm voice broke through her reverie. "Mr. Fitzhugh says we're almost there. And then it's right to bed with you. You're white as a sheet."

Mary flashed her a grateful smile. Thank God for Jan. Despite her earlier misgivings, without Jan's practical cheerfulness, she would have been totally alone. Jan had become more of a friend than a nurse and the only constant in Mary's rapidly changing world. She was tired, and more than a little frightened. Trust Jan to sense that. Resolutely she tried to concentrate on the present, but even as she did so, the car turned off the main road and started up the long, tree-lined drive that led to the main house, and in spite of herself she remembered the first time she had come this way—so long ago—when she was seventeen.

Was it only nine years ago? Her father had died that spring, and Stan was on assignment in Africa, so she was living alone, going to business school and working part time as a florist's helper to make ends meet. In fact, she remembered ruefully she had only been working a week when she had been promoted to driving the delivery van; a rather dubious honor, since she was not that confident a driver and the manual transmission demanded her total concentration.

Perhaps that was why when she was pulling into the circular drive at the front entrance to the Fitzhugh mansion, coming to a very jerky stop, she collided with the sleek, low-slung sports car that was already there.

"Oh, no," she wailed in fright and anger at the clumsiness that she was sure was about to cost her her new job.

To make matters worse, the white sports car was not empty, but contained a man and woman locked in a very torrid embrace at the exact moment of impact. In fact, watching that embrace, just a little enviously, had no doubt been a major factor in causing the accident.

She sat frozen behind the wheel of the van as a tall man of incredible good looks and righteous anger at having been interrupted at such a sensitive moment untangled himself reluctantly from his luscious companion and strode toward the van.

"Okay, buddy, where did you get your driver's license?" he demanded as he flung open the door on the driver's side.

Large terror-stricken blue eyes stared into his furious gray ones. The expression in the gray eyes changed from anger to surprise as he took a careful inventory of the errant driver—a young girl with enormous frightened eyes set in a freshly scrubbed face with moist trembling lips.

"Are you even old enough to drive?" he said in a much gentler tone.

"Yes...y-yes, sir." Her voice quavered and her body was stiff behind her fastened seat belt. "H-have I done much damage to your car?" The words tumbled out with difficulty, and she held her breath for the obvious answer; she could see the dent that had crumpled the expensive fender. She would lose her job for sure now. Her hands gripped the steering wheel in despair. "It was my fault," she admitted, "I was looking...that is, I was thinking..." She floundered in red-faced confusion.

"Hey"—his hands reached out and grasped her trembling shoulders, shaking her gently— "it's all right." His strong fingers dug deeply into her soft skin, liking the feel of her, and almost imperceptibly, his grip softened and became sensual, caressing. His eyes, no longer amused, were as surprised as her own at the current of awareness that was passing between them.

"What on earth is a delivery truck doing at the front entrance?" a sharp female voice broke through their trancelike fixation with each other. It was the woman whose passionate embrace had just been interrupted and she was not the least happy about it. Jamie Fitzhugh had been about to propose, of that she was certain, and the person responsible for breaking into that long-planned-for moment would definitely suffer for it. "I think we should call the police and have this wreck towed away," she sneered.

"Oh, no. Please." Mary cast a desperate glance from one to the other of them.

"Miriam, for heaven's sake. Can't you see the kid's scared to death?" His arm circled Mary's shoulder. "Come into the house, honey," he soothed. "You need a drink to settle your nerves. Then we can talk about the damage to our cars."

"I'm n-not old enough to drink," she stuttered. "Besides, I'm supposed to be d-delivering f-flowers for a p-party." She pointed to the huge bouquets of gladioli in the back of the van.

Effortlessly he reached back and picked up one basket, which he handed to the astonished Miriam, then picked up the remaining two, one in each hand, and jumped down from the van. With an imperious nod he indicated that Mary should precede him into the house.

Barbara had been the housekeeper even then, and she came out to meet them—a small, fragile woman in her mid-thirties, and very beautiful. She stood in the doorway and, at Jamie's terse command, moved quickly to lead Mary into the house and a comfortable chair. Then she discreetly disappeared, taking the flowers with her.

The rest of the afternoon was a blur of jumbled, precious memories. When she would not accept a drink, Jamie had thrust coffee and sandwiches upon her, sitting with her, watching her eat, calming her fears of losing her job, and saying silly things to make her laugh.

He insisted that she was too shaken to drive the beat-up old van; therefore, he should drive while she made the rest of her floral deliveries. Helping her had started out as a lark on an otherwise boring afternoon, but they were soon engrossed in the wonder of discovering each other. Somewhere along the way Miriam disappeared from the scene and was never heard from again.

Mary learned that Jamie was an only son, twenty-four, and single; that besides being a junior partner in a law firm, he was also associated in business with his father. Mary had never paid any attention to the social caste of the area, but the huge mansion she had just seen told her how successful he was.

Jamie learned that she was only seventeen, that she lived alone in a small house her father had left her, and that she was working part-time while she attended business school. Though she had a brother somewhere in Africa, she seldom saw or heard from him and was literally alone in the world.

It was inevitable that he should kiss her. It started out as a salute to her youth and pluck and quickly became much more as he discovered an untapped dimension of emotion in her budding body and an overwhelming compulsion within him to explore that dimension. With her moist, promising kisses clinging to his lips, he knew immediately that she needed someone to look after her and protect her; and it was inconceivable to him that anyone but himself could be entrusted with that responsibility.

They saw each other every day after that. He took her to expensive restaurants and the opera and the theater and the ball park. Often she cooked simple meals for him in her home, and he helped her do the dishes afterward and then they watched TV on her small set or took walks in the nearby park. Some nights he would bring briefs from the office to work on while she did her homework. He encouraged her to pursue her studies, and she brought him her report cards like a child wanting to make him a gift of her good grades and anxious to please.

He gave her praise and passion and purpose as he became everything to her—friend and family and lover. They had known each other six months when, on her eighteenth birthday, he asked her to marry him and accompany him to Greece. On their wedding night she knew why she had been born.

As the car rounded the curve of the circular drive and drew to a halt before the imposing gray stone mansion, Mary stole a quick look sideways at Jamie's stern profile. His face was older now and each one of those nine years had left lines around his mouth and eyes. Was he remembering, as she was, the wide-eyed young girl who had crashed into his life on that summer day so long ago?

Her mouth tightened. Of course not. This man was a stranger to the laughing Jamie who had gathered her so completely into his life. She thought then that she had stolen his heart; she knew now that she had merely borrowed it. Determined to remember this, she looked away from him quickly.

The car came to a halt in front of the entrance and instantly the door opened and her worst fears were realized. Barbara stood there, waiting to greet them. Her tiny figure was encased in a sensible navy dress that nevertheless managed to emphasize her lush bosom and her deep auburn hair, which showed no trace of gray in its sleek french twist. She was at least forty-five years old now but easily looked fifteen years younger. Her past indiscretions had not left a mark on her attractive features.

She stepped forward as Jan was fumbling with the folding wheelchair. "May I help?" Her voice was polite, but she avoided looking directly at Mary.

However, before the chair could be readied, Jamie scooped Mary up in his arms and headed into the house. "Never mind that, Mrs. Wright. It will be quicker if I just carry her in. Just bring the chair so that it will be handy for her use later on." He carried Mary past Barbara, holding her tightly against the rock-hard wall of his chest. Mary was too surprised by his action to do more than cling helplessly against him, her elbow crooked around his neck for balance while her bandaged hands were held gingerly away from him.

The warmth of his hands gripping her just under her knees and biting into her waist radiated a flustering warmth throughout her body. Her breasts were flattened against his chest, and her cheek lay tentatively against the thick column of his neck. She knew from the steady beat of the pulse there that, unlike her, he was not in any way affected by this first physical contact between them in four years. Blood roared in her ears until she thought she would faint.

"Please," she managed, "put me down."

"I've arranged a light lunch," Barbara said, following close behind them, taking quick, hurried steps to keep pace with Jamie's long strides so that she could listen to their conversation. "Why don't you take her right into the dining room?"

"No!" The protest was automatic. She would not eat in their presence while they watched Jan feed her. It was humiliating enough to be so dependent; she couldn't let them—Jamie and Barbara—see how utterly helpless she now was.

Jamie did not slacken his pace but looked over his shoulder at Barbara with an impatient scowl. "I'm taking her directly to her room. Send Mrs. Wright in with a tray for her and then find Cal. Why isn't he here? I expected him to be waiting for us."

Barbara hesitated for a moment and then hurried to catch up with him again. "I'll bring the tray myself," she offered helpfully.

Mary stiffened, and as though he knew what she was thinking, Jamie stopped dead in his tracks, turning abruptly to face Barbara, who, surprised at his action, almost collided into them.

"You have things to do around the house, I'm sure, Barb. Mrs. Wright is being paid to look after my wife, so let's leave her to her job, shall we?" To soften the harshness of his command, he flashed her a half smile. "You can feed me, if you like. Cal and I will join you for lunch as soon as he's talked to his mother."

Still Barbara hesitated, as though she were loath to leave them alone; but when he raised one eyebrow in a silent command, she turned away reluctantly and allowed him to proceed down the hall without further interruption.

At the end of the hall an open door beckoned, and he carried her through it into a large airy bedroom. He walked over to an easy chair that faced a wide sunny window overlooking the grounds and lowered her carefully into it. "Welcome home, Mrs. Fitzhugh."

She looked up quickly at the bitterness in his voice. His features were bland but there was no mistaking the ironic glitter in his eyes.

"This wasn't my idea," she defended herself. "The last place I want to be is here. And—and perhaps I won't stay after all," she added in a wavering voice.

His long fingers reached out and cupped her chin in a fierce, cruel gesture. "Oh, yes, you will, Mrs. Fitzhugh. History will not repeat itself. You're here now and here you will stay until I say differently."

"You can't keep me here against my will," she choked.

He did not bother to answer, but his eyes mocked her, and she knew a moment of pure terror. She was completely helpless, and now that he had her in this house, there was no one she could turn to for help. She had been a fool to leave the safety of the hospital. "I—I'm going to tell Jan I want to return to the hospital,'' she warned. At that, he actually smiled, and she looked away in despair. Of course. Jan worked for him.

He released his painful hold on her chin and slipped into the chair across from her, crossing his long legs and resting one hand on his knee. ''You and I are prime examples of that old chestnut about politics making strange bedfellows. I'm afraid we're stuck with each other.'' He gave her another of those chilling smiles that frightened her so. ''It can be as pleasant or as painful as you make it.''

''W-what do you m-mean?''

He threw his hands up in a wide sweeping gesture. ''Simple, really. The voters want to see us as one big happy family. As long as you do nothing to destroy that image, there's no reason why we can't share the same house like two civilized people.'' She opened her mouth to protest, but he waved her objections aside.

''For now, that will consist simply of one or two newspaper interviews, but within a month, when you've fully recovered from your injuries, I will expect you to accompany me on some speaking tours.''

''And I suppose you expect me to make speeches on your behalf.'' Her sarcasm was undisguised.

''Hardly. Any speeches in this family will be made by me. All you will have to do is flash that two-faced smile of yours on cue.''

She let that remark pass. ''You'd do anything — use anybody — to get elected, wouldn't you?''

He rose angrily and walked away from her to

look out into the spring garden. "Do you think I like this? Nothing would please me more than to just present myself to the voters and take my chances. Unfortunately, your reappearance on the scene has made that impossible. In order to get on with the important issues in this campaign, I first have to get you off my back." He turned back angrily to face her. "You agreed to all of this last week. Why are you talking about leaving now? Are you trying to hold me up for money or something?"

Mary's eyes flashed as furiously as his. "Oh, no, you don't. Any blackmail going on around here isn't being done by me!"

"What the hell is that supposed to mean?"

She opened her mouth to shout back at him when she saw the boy standing in the doorway, staring at them with shocked eyes. The concern in Mary's face caused Jamie to turn in that direction. He held out his hand, and the boy hurried to his side.

Mother and son stared at each other. The warm, wondering look in Mary's eyes met open antagonism.

"Hello, Cal," she managed breathlessly, opening her arms to him.

He took a quick step backward, almost hiding behind his father. "Hello, ma'am." Her arms fell woodenly to her side. Ma'am?

Jamie's eyes went back and forth between the two of them and for a moment Mary saw a flicker of compassion in their fog-gray depths. "Kiss your mother hello," he commanded gently.

The boy gulped and took a hesitant step forward, his hands digging deeply into the pockets of his jeans. Mary's eyes roamed over him. He was such a handsome boy. His jeans were mud-spattered and his plaid shirt had several buttons undone and one shirttail had slipped out, but his sandy hair was wet and lay in damp curls on his collar and his face had a just-scrubbed look that proclaimed that he had tried to make himself presentable.

Jamie nudged him again, and he took the last two steps that brought him directly in front of her. He bent forward stiffly at the waist and gave her a quick, shuddering kiss on the cheek before he straightened and moved back to his father's side. Her bandaged hand went up to rest where his kiss had been and she could almost feel its warmth through the thick layers of gauze.

"Your front teeth have grown in," she said inanely, breaking the heavy silence.

He gave her a questioning look.

"The picture I saw of you," she hurried on to explain, "the one your grandfather showed me. Your two front teeth were missing in the picture. But they've grown in beautifully, haven't they?"

He stood staring at her. His eyes never left her face, but his hand crept into his father's as if to show her where his allegiance lay.

"They're very nice teeth." She could not stop herself from babbling. This was her baby and her arms ached to hold him, yet there he stood, shifting uncomfortably from one leg to the other, looking for an excuse to leave. She kept talking, hoping to keep him in the same room just a little longer. However, his father released him from his torment.

"Barbara is holding lunch for you, Son. Run along, and I'll join you in a while."

"Oh." Mary could not conceal her disappointment as he practically ran out of the room.

Jamie gave her a long mocking look, reminding her that her maternal concern was four years too late. "Don't worry, he'll be back," he announced magnanimously. "I've arranged for him to visit you each day for an hour in the afternoon. If we're going to be living together for the next six months, it will make things much easier for all of us if you and Cal become better acquainted."

Mary gave him a thin defiant smile. So she was to be allowed to see her son an hour a day, was she. Obviously Jamie did not consider her any threat for their son's affections and he could afford to be generous. Still, she clutched at even that small concession. It was a beginning, and if she and Cal saw each other every day, perhaps she could convince him that she was not the monster Jamie had made her out to be; perhaps she could still win her son back.

As if reading her thoughts, Jamie interrupted savagely. "I've told Cal that you are just going to be here for six months and that after the election you will probably be moving on. He realizes that you will only be here temporarily and he accepts that. I don't want you to do or say anything to give him the impression that it could become something more permanent. I won't have you hurt him the way ... I won't have you hurt him," he finished with grim finality.

She was saved from answering this latest attack by the appearance of Jan with a luncheon tray. With a curt nod in Jan's direction and not another word to Mary, Jamie turned on his heel and left the room. However, the violence of his unspoken threat remained behind to torment her.

Chapter Four

Mary stared at the door that closed behind Jamie until the last echo of his footsteps had faded away. Then she turned with a resigned sigh to face Jan and the despised luncheon tray.

"I'm really not hungry," she tried to protest, but Jan would not be put off.

"Nonsense. Of course you are. It's just more of your foolishness about not wanting me to feed you. I thought we had thrashed that all out by now. You have to eat. You can't feed yourself. I'm here to help you," she repeated in her schoolteacher-to-difficult-student tone of voice. "Now, open your mouth."

In spite of herself, Mary smiled and did as she was told. Jan could be very bossy and though she hated the helplessness that forced her to endure being fed like a baby, there was nothing to be gained by protesting. Instead, she concentrated on eating as quickly as possible, barely tasting the food, in an effort to get the odious chore over with.

When Jan was satisfied that she had eaten

enough, the tray was put aside, and with gentle hands she helped Mary to undress and slip into the waiting bed. She was so compassionate in her ministrations that for a moment Mary was tempted to believe that Jamie had been mistaken in his belief that Jan would not help her to leave here if she so desired. As Jan slipped a clean satin nightgown over her head, Mary put this theory to a test.

"Jan, I think it may have been a mistake for me to come here, and I wondered if you could see about getting me readmitted to the hospital."

Jan's friendly face was distressed. "Why ever would you want to do a thing like that, Mary? This is such a lovely place. I'm sure you'll get well so much faster here."

Mary sighed. So, it was true; she was a prisoner in this huge, unfriendly house. And yet . . .

Cal was here. In spite of everything, there was no way she would have left this house, even if Jan had offered to help her, as long as there was a chance to be near him. Somehow she would turn her confinement into an opportunity to make friends with him. And after that . . . well, she would see. Just thinking of Cal, knowing he was somewhere in this house, knowing she would see him again soon, filled her with a warm glow. She settled down to rest, and just before she fell asleep, she allowed herself a smile of anticipation.

The whispering woke her, but she did not open her eyes. She recognized Cal's voice and she lay there, pretending to be asleep, so that she would not frighten him off.

"Shhh, don't make so much noise. You'll wake her up."

"She's pretty," a lisping little-girl voice stated in awe. "She doesn't look like a wicked witch at all, Cal. She looks like Goldilocks!"

"Well, she's a witch," he whispered back angrily, "and you're just a stupid girl and I'm sorry I even brought you in to see her."

"Don't be mad at me, Cal," the sweet little voice whimpered. "I just said she was pretty. But I promise not to like her if you don't want me to."

"Well, okay, then. Just remember that pretty is as pretty does. Didn't your mom tell us that? And didn't she tell us that she ran off and left me, just like the wicked stepmother left Hansel and Gretel in the woods, hoping they would die?" His whisper was hard and accusing.

"But you didn't die," she chirped up happily. "You came to live in Fitz's house, and then I was borned, and now we're all family. Family," she repeated proudly, "and my mommy and your daddy both say that you must always take care of me and never be mad at me," she reminded him petulantly.

"Be quiet, Jaycie," he whispered sternly. "If you want me to look after you, just you mind me. Now, let's go. You're so noisy, it's a wonder you haven't wakened her already."

"Maybe she needs to be kissed by a handsome prince," Jaycie suggested innocently, drawing on her storybook references.

"What are you two doing in here?"

The unexpected addition of a loud, shrill voice

to the two childish whispers caused Mary's eyes to fly open in surprise. She found herself staring into her son's startled eyes, which widened into frightened shock as he realized that she was awake. He grasped the wrist of the little girl standing next to him and they fairly flew out of the room, but not before Mary had had a good look at his companion—a chubby-cheeked, sandy-haired child who was the image of Cal at the same age. The resemblance was unmistakable.

In that one moment the fantasy she had begun to weave around her son came crashing down around her ears. Their childish whispers had left her no doubts as to Cal's opinion of her, and the sight of little Jaycie had reopened the old wounds that had sent her rushing into the night four years ago. She turned with dull resignation in the direction of the voice that had sent the children scurrying and found Barbara staring down at her.

"Awake, are you? Perhaps this would be a good time for us to talk."

"I've nothing to say to you." Mary turned her face to the wall.

"If you're going to be here awhile, we're going to have to get our stories straight," Barbara insisted. "What have you told Jamie?"

"I haven't discussed you with Jamie, if that's what you mean." Mary turned back to face her with scornful eyes. Was it her imagination, or did Barbara seem to breathe a sigh of relief?

"I thought not. It's just as well. There's nothing to tell now, anyway."

"He never did marry you, did he?" Mary could not resist that one sharp jab to assuage her own pain.

"Of course not." The housekeeper's lips twisted with bitterness. "The Fitzhughs do not divorce. Remember? Well, Fitz did not divorce for me, and..." She hesitated. "And neither did Jamie."

"And yet you're still *friends* with father and son," Mary taunted.

"No." The denial was so abrupt and so bitter that Mary knew she was telling the truth. "Fitz was through with me long before Jaycie was born—that was Jaycie who just raced out of here with Cal—and Jamie has gone on to other women, too.

"You would never have held on to him, you know," she taunted maliciously. "He's like his father. Women go in and out of his life through a constantly revolving door. If it hadn't been me, it would have been someone else." Her shrill voice rose defensively. "You would have left him eventually over a woman, just as his mother left his father."

"That's comforting to know," Mary responded dryly. "I'm sure it eases your conscience to think so. What I can't understand is why you are still here if both your former lovers have discarded you. Don't you feel a bit de trop?"

Barbara's lips curved into a contemptuous sneer. "You are naive, aren't you? I believe in being practical, myself. When I lost their sexual interest, I concentrated on making myself indispensable to them in the running of this house, and long ago relinquished any personal claim on either of them. Everything runs smoothly here, and their comings and goings are never criticized. Why should they get rid of me? Besides," she added with bright, hard eyes, "my daughter has a right to be brought up in this house. And I have no intention of leaving just because you are back," she added in defiance.

Mary stared at her in amazement. She could never hope to understand the workings of a mind like Barbara's; but surely it must be obvious, even to her, that Mary could never be a threat to her. "Just stay out of my way, Barb. You and I have nothing to talk about."

For the first time the other woman was ill at ease. "The fact is, we do," she faltered. "Jamie is about to establish a trust fund for Jaycie. I wouldn't want him to change his mind because of your return."

"Then perhaps you shouldn't have brought the matter up," Mary snapped. "Don't you know that if I thought I could do anything to hurt you, I would?"

The housekeeper bit her lip. "As a woman, I expect you would. As a mother, I was hoping you would realize that Jaycie is innocent and shouldn't be used as a way of getting back at me. She has a birthright due her, and I'm asking you not to try and take it away from her. Be good to her," Barbara pleaded slyly, "as I've been good to your son these past four years."

Mary sneered. "So I've heard—telling him that his mother deserted him." She watched Barbara

pale as her jab struck home, but she was too dis-
heartened to take pleasure in her discomfort.
"Well, you needn't worry, Barb. I won't do or say
anything to upset your apple cart. I have no intention of ever discussing you or your child with
Jamie. And whether or not he supports her is no
concern of mine. Actually, I suppose it is the least
he can do under the circumstances. However, do
us both a favor and stay away from me. I'm afraid
I'm not as easygoing as Fitz and Jamie; and you
are not 'indispensable' to me."

Finding herself dismissed with these words, the
elegant housekeeper left the room before Mary
could change her mind, closing the door behind
her with a triumphant click. She had gotten what
she came for and nothing else mattered.

Still numb from the encounter, Mary watched
her leave. Long minutes after she had gone, Mary
continued to stare at the closed door that separated her from the rest of the house. In spite of
herself, she had been forced to remember another time, another closed door that Barbara had
opened.

Mary had been in their bedroom, sleeping off the
lazy aftermath of lovemaking. The sound of the
door opening had awakened her, and she stretched
out a lazy hand, searching for Jamie, only to encounter the empty pillow where his head had lain.
She opened her eyes, disappointed but not surprised. Jamie had mentioned that he was returning to the office. She stretched and smiled lazily,

remembering the things he had done to her, that she had done to him.

Her smile grew as though she were hoarding a secret, and then she noticed that Barbara had entered the room and was carrying Jamie's soaked suit coat gingerly in front of her by the fingertips, and her eyes had been cold and almost resentfully accusing.

"Haven't you any shame?" Barb blurted out. "Jamie's clothes are floating all over the pool, and the grocery boy is giggling like a fool as he helps Mrs. Barnes fish them out."

Mary's lips refused to relinquish their smile. "It isn't the first time," she teased as she sat up in the wide bed, pulling the sheet up to cover herself as she did so. "But don't worry—they know we're married."

"Oh, I forgot," Barbara's voice was bitter. "The Fitzhughs can do anythng they want, can't they?"

This time Mary gave her a closer look. It was not like Barbara to be so edgy. Since Cal's birth, she and Barb had been thrown together often. One day a week Fitz had his housekeeper/mistress pick up Cal to spend the afternoon with him, and on these occasions the two women had become casual friends. That Barb was Fitz's current mistress as well as his housekeeper was no secret, but it was tactfully never discussed. They were not that good friends.

"Is something wrong, Barb?" Mary asked with sudden concern. "Where's Cal?"

The hard light in Barbara's eyes glittered more furiously at the mention of Cal's name. "Oh, don't worry about the precious Fitzhugh heir. He's downstairs with Mrs. Barnes. He thinks it's very funny that his daddy left all his clothes in the swimming pool."

"Oh, don't be so stuffy, Barb." Mary tried to coax a smile from her friend. Now that she knew Cal was all right, she could joke again. "Haven't you ever been in love?"

Something inside of Barbara seemed to snap. Pure venom was in the glance she directed at the sensuous figure on the bed who seemed so smug in her own happiness.

"No, I'm just pregnant, that's all!"

"Oh, Barb." Mary reached a sympathetic hand out to her. "I'm sorry. Is it Fitz—" She knew she had said too much. They *never* discussed Fitz in that way. "I'm sorry," she repeated awkwardly.

"What has Fitz to do with it?" Barb asked in a cold fury.

"Why, I—" Mary was disconcerted. She knew Barb was upset, but her hostility was unexpected, as though she blamed Mary for being happily married while she... "I'm sorry," she apologized again, not sure what she was apologizing for.

"Well, save your sympathy. Don't patronize me because you think you have the world's most perfect husband."

"I—I'm not," Mary protested, still wondering why she was under attack.

"Because you don't," Barbara continued spitefully. "Your 'perfect' husband is the father of my baby!'' She blurted the words out quickly and then looked stunned at what she had said.

Time hung suspended, and the silence in the room threatened to destroy them both.

"Don't be silly," Mary managed at last. "Everyone knows that you and Fitz—"

Barbara was laughing wildly. "What's the matter, don't you think what's good enough for Fitz is good enough for his son?"

The room spun dizzily, and Mary fought hard to keep from fainting. "It's not true. It couldn't be. Jamie loves me. He spends every free minute with me. There wouldn't even be time," she was thinking aloud.

Again that wild, half-crazed laugh. "You're such a little fool. What do you know about satisfying a man? Would you like me to tell you the sort of things your husband likes that you don't know anything about?"

Mary's hands flew to her ears. "I won't listen." But it was no use and she was forced to listen as Barbara described in detail ways of pleasing a man sexually that she had, indeed, never heard of. Twisted, perverted things that could not possibly apply to her Jamie.

"... and as for when," the taunting voice went on, "dear, dutiful Jamie stops by to see the great Fitz every night, doesn't he, while you put Cal to bed? Only he doesn't spend all that time with Fitz. He spends it with me."

"Why are you saying these things?" Mary screamed. "They aren't true. I know they aren't."

"You'd like to believe that, wouldn't you?"

Barb hurled back at her. "Well, I'm sick of storybook princesses who think they can have everything. Why should you live in a dreamworld while the rest of us have to face harsh reality? Right now, you think your child is the heir to the Fitzhugh fortune, but soon my son will be born, and he'll be more of a Fitzhugh than Cal!"

Barbara threw the wet jacket she was still holding down on the bed with a vengeance. "Now, when you have your next romantic interlude in the pool, maybe you'll think about what I've just told you; and perhaps you won't feel so damn smug and secure. Why should you have your perfect little world when mine is shattered!" Sobbing, she turned and ran out of the room, slamming the door behind her. Mary lay there, stunned, clinging to the wet jacket.

Later, when she reexamined the situation, she thought that perhaps if that afternoon with Jamie had not been so perfect, the knowledge of his infidelity would not have hurt so much. But after the heights of ecstasy that she had known that day, it was impossible for her to live with the hell that Barbara's revelation brought with it. She could not accept it and retain her sanity.

In her bewildered mind the only solution had been to leave.

She wrote Jamie a note, saying that she would be staying at the Alemeda Plaza for a few days to think things over—she could not even bring herself to put into words what these things were—and then she had packed her overnight case and left, stopping only long enough to kiss Cal and to tell Mrs. Barnes to stay with him until his father came home.

In all honesty she had never expected to leave for good. Of course, Jamie would come after her, and they would talk it out and he would explain everything. Barbara would be proved a liar, and they would resume their life as though none of this had happened.

Only it had not worked out like that. Jamie had not tried to get in touch with her. She had not seen nor heard from him until that day in the hospital after the fire. She would not have known what to do, where to turn, if she had not found Stan's letter in her purse.

She had been going to share its contents with Jamie that afternoon, but their lovemaking had pushed it to the back of her mind, and he had left before she could bring it up afterward. Her brother was back in the country and anxious to see her. She had looked forward to introducing him to her husband, but instead she went to see Stan alone and bitter, and he had taken her in.

Stan had urged her to contact her husband and attempt a reconciliation, but her humiliation and sense of rejection was too deep. Jamie had known where she was staying, that she was waiting to hear from him, and he had ignored her. That, in itself, convinced her that Barbara's story was true and that he had been looking for an excuse to leave her. Their marriage was over.

Staring at the door through which Barbara had just exited, Mary was beyond tears. How quickly

the winds of fortune changed. Once Barbara had
accused her of being a storybook princess who
had everything; now Barbara was firmly established as the mistress of this house and the
mother of Jamie's child, and she, Mary, was on
the outside looking in.

Running away had accomplished nothing. She
was right back where she had started, and this
time she had no choice but to face the unpleasant
facts of life she had tried so hard to avoid. Well,
she told herself firmly, if nothing else, those four
years on her own had changed her from a naive,
lost fool to a coldly practical woman who was better able to deal with the Jamies and Barbaras of
this world. The trick was not to allow herself to
feel anything. Only then could she be sure they
would not hurt her again, and she had had plenty
of time to learn that trick well.

Only Cal mattered to her now, and perhaps it
was too late even for that.

The days that followed soon fell into a pattern.
The mornings were reserved for bed baths and
physical therapy. The bed baths were a nuisance
but necessary to keep the bandages on Mary's
hands from getting wet. The physical therapy,
which consisted of changing the bandages, apply-
ing medication, and exercising her fingers and her
leg, was a torturous process designed to overcome
the infection and to restore the use of her ex-
tremities, although both Jan and the doctor were
bluntly pessimistic as to the outcome.

Mary had been told that there was a strong possibility she would not make a full recovery. The scar tissue could make her fingers stiff and useless, and the infection in her leg wound threatened to become gangrenous. They did not have to say more to get her compliance to any treatment they suggested. The fear of remaining helpless under the Fitzhugh roof was a sword of Damocles over her head that had to be overcome.

Anything they told Mary to do she did without complaint. The exercises were painful, but she insisted that they be done for even longer periods than the doctor recommended. The medication that ate away the infection was caustic, but she accepted the pain stoically. The only thing she insisted upon was that no one other than Jan be present during the treatments to overhear the small moans that sometimes found their way past her lips. The bedroom door was carefully locked before the start of each session to insure that they would not be interrupted by unwelcome visitors.

Jan prided herself on being objective where her patients were concerned, but often she found herself reacting emotionally to Mary's suffering, and she found herself regarding the younger woman more as a sister than a patient. Neither of them said anything during the treatments, but Jan worked as quickly and as efficiently as possible to bring them to a rapid conclusion. When they were done, she would bathe Mary's face with cool towels to wipe away the perspiration and tears while Mary sank into an exhausted sleep.

By the end of the first week, it was obvious that the treatments were working. When the doctor confirmed what they both felt, the women accepted his findings with triumphant smiles and pursued their objective with even more zeal. The pain was still there, and in the mornings the bedroom door remained locked to outsiders, but a goal was in sight and they worked confidently toward it.

After that first day, there were few visitors to concern themselves with. Barbara kept her distance. If there were household arrangements to be discussed, she talked to Jan, who relayed the information to Mary. Jamie had not been to see her since he carried her into the bedroom over a week ago, and Mary did not ask anyone where he was.

Surprisingly, Fitz was a regular visitor. He would stop in each evening before dinner and stay about five minutes. He would ask how she was feeling without really listening to her answer, and then he would nod his head and hurry away. She was here and that was enough for him.

Her former employer, Mr. Evans, called faithfully each evening, and they talked about the people in the office and light items in the newspaper that he had selected to amuse her. He mentioned visiting her but was hesitant to come to the Fitzhugh mansion, and she did not encourage him. Still, his phone calls were pleasant, and Mary found herself looking forward to them, even though she could not even hold the phone and had to depend upon Jan to do that for her.

But the highlight of her day was Cal's visit. He came dutifully each day after school, even though it was obvious that he would rather have been anyplace else. After several futile attempts to draw him out in conversation in his first visit, Mary gave up and suggested that he could leave early to play with his friends. As tempting as the offer obviously was to him, he surprised her by refusing.

"Dad says I'm to stay an hour," he reminded her solemnly. After another long silence between them, he cleared his throat and asked if he could watch cartoons on the TV. "I don't think Dad would mind if I did that," he reasoned.

Of course Mary agreed, but it was disappointing not to be talking to him, learning to know him. Still, he was in the same room, and she satisfied herself with watching him as he demolished the cookies and milk that Jan routinely set before him. At the end of the cartoon show he rose, telling time as children will by the TV. "Hour's up," he announced, and as though that said it all, he left the room. The next day at the same time he was back to eat cookies and watch cartoons, and their routine was established.

Until the day he brought Jaycie with him. "Jaycie's mom had to run an errand. I told her I would keep an eye on Jaycie," he explained.

"Oh, but—" Mary was appalled. Surely *that* child was not going to intrude upon the one hour of the day she looked forward to.

"She won't be any trouble," Cal said, sensing her dismay, "and she can share my cookies."

"I won't be any trouble," Jaycie repeated solemnly, slipping her hand into Cal's for reassurance, as she, too, sensed Mary's displeasure.

Tears of frustration welled unshed in the corners of Mary's eyes. "I'm sorry..." Her voice wobbled. "It just wouldn't—"

"You hate Jaycie, don't you?" her son accused. "Barbara said you wouldn't want her here. Why? She hasn't done anything." He stared at his mother in childish anger.

It was the first emotion he had shown in all the times he had visited her, and all in defense of— Mary's heart sank as she watched him holding on to Jaycie, whose little face was contorted in a prelude to tears.

"Why doesn't she like me, Cal?" Two fat tears slid down her chubby cheeks, enraging Cal.

"I told you she was mean. Come on, let's go. I don't care what Dad says!"

"Oh, wait." Cal mustn't leave like this, hating her. She lifted a hand helplessly to stop them. What on earth was wrong with her, blaming the child because of what her parents were—who her parents were? Even Cal knew better than that. In a perverse way she was proud of the way he defended the little girl against her senseless prejudice.

"I want you both to stay," she forced herself to say. "Jan, will you get them some more milk and cookies?" It was all the encouragement Jan needed to head for the kitchen.

Mollified, the two youngsters turned on the TV and sat cross-legged on the floor to watch the cartoons. Mary sank back in her chair, limp with relief and despair and studied them. Did anyone else notice the remarkable resemblance between the two children, or was it only to her—seeing Cal as he had been at three—that the sandy curls and gray eyes took on such a special significance?

The next day the children came together again and after that, Mary resigned herself to the fact that if she wanted to see her son, she would have to see the two of them. She did not mind. In a way Jaycie's presence had broken the ice. Where once the hour had passed in silence, except for the sounds from the TV, now the two children chattered incessantly and occasionally they would turn in her direction to have an argument settled or an action on the screen explained. At last her son was talking to her. She was not a friend, but she was no longer his enemy.

"Why don't you have some cookies, too?" Jaycie asked curiously one afternoon, lifting a half-eaten cookie up to share with Mary.

"Don't be silly," Cal answered for her. "Can't you see she can't hold anything with her hands bandaged like that?" He looked at his mother in sudden comprehension. "Is that why you don't come down to the dining room, ma'am? I thought it was because you didn't like—" He turned away without finishing the sentence.

Mary was at a loss for words. How could she explain to a child how useless she felt with her bandaged hands? How could he understand how lonely she was in this alien house, which sheltered him so lovingly? When she said nothing, he pursued the subject doggedly. "Who feeds you?"

"Jan helps me," she admitted awkwardly. "Now, stop all this chatter and finish your snack."

"Let me feed her. Let me," Jaycie chimed in, and before anyone could stop her, she had climbed on Mary's lap, banging Mary's sore leg in the process. "Open wide," she coaxed sweetly.

Despite the pain in her leg, Mary found herself laughing and taking a bite of the proffered cookie. But when Jaycie would have given her another taste, she turned her head aside with a laughing "Enough."

She expected that Jaycie would climb down off her lap and return to Cal's side, but instead the child's tiny arms wound themselves around her neck as she fitted herself against Mary's tense body. "You smell nice," Jaycie observed as she cuddled closer. "Not like a wicked witch at all."

"Jaycie!" Cal's face went red with embarrassment as he tugged the little girl off his mother's lap and hurriedly left the room, pulling her reluctantly after him.

With a trace of a smile hovering over her lips, Mary watched them go. The feel of the child's arms around her neck was still warm in her memory, and it was impossible to connect her in any way to the collapse of her marriage. Jaycie had managed to wiggle her way into Mary's affections and there was no removing her now. In fact, Mary reminded herself ruefully, Jaycie's arms around her neck had been the only friendly gesture made to her in this hostile place.

"I guess you're not the wicked witch I thought you were, either," she whispered under her breath after the departing child.

Chapter Five

If Herbert Evans had called at his usual hour instead of before breakfast, they would have remembered to lock the door. If it had not been a Saturday, the children would have been occupied elsewhere at that hour. As it was, the phone rang just as Jan was walking over to lock the door, and she turned back to answer the phone and then held it while Mary chatted with her former employer. At the end of the conversation, the door forgotten, the two women started on their daily ritual of exercise.

Mary's hands were carefully unbandaged and the raw red skin heavily lubricated with a rich lotion that softened the skin as the fingers were bent and exercised. They were becoming more flexible every day, but still the scarred tissue resisted their efforts and did not lend itself easily to the movements the two women relentlessly demanded of it. Without conscious thought on Mary's part, tears of protest fell down her cheeks as they worked, and her breath came in short, labored gasps.

To Cal, standing in the doorway of the half-opened door, with Jaycie in tow as usual, the scene was one of medieval torture, and Mary was the victim. After staring with horrified eyes while the nurse seemingly twisted Mary's hands in a deliberate effort to cause her pain, he ran out of the room and down the hall, calling to his father for help.

"Dad. Dad. Come quick. Mrs. Wright is hurting her!"

And Jaycie came trailing after him, screaming, "Mary's crying. Mary's crying. Mary's crying."

The sight of the two hysterical children bursting into his room stopped Jamie in the midst of shaving. Hurriedly he dabbed the shaving cream away with an impatient flick of the towel on his shoulders and turned toward them. He couldn't get a coherent sentence out of either child, so he allowed himself to be led down the hall to Mary's room.

At the sight of him standing in her room, clad only in a towel around his waist, Jan and Mary stopped what they were doing like two guilty children caught in the midst of a forbidden act. His sharp eyes swept over both of them, summing up the scene in a quick glance. He lingered a long moment over the ugly red scar tissue of Mary's hands before raising his glance to her tear-stained face.

"Does that feel as bad as it looks?" he choked hoarsely.

Mary threw a desperate look to Jan, who immediately wiped Mary's face dry with the towel that was waiting there for just that purpose. "If we could be alone, Mr. Fitzhugh," the nurse said in her most professional manner, "I'll be finished here in a few minutes."

"If it was privacy you wanted, perhaps you should have locked the door," he countered in his most autocratic manner. "As it is, you have frightened the children." He knelt in front of his son and Jaycie and patted each child on the shoulder in a tender gesture that was entirely at odds with his demeanor toward the women. "Everything is all right here. Run along and play."

"She was crying," Cal contradicted. "Mrs. Wright was hurting her." His accusation demanded that the nurse be punished.

"Your mother is fine, Son," Jamie repeated patiently. "Sometimes when you're ill, it has to hurt a little before it gets better. Like when you broke your wrist. Remember how you flinched when they set it? But it was all right after they finished, wasn't it? Well, your mother will be fine, too. Go out and play." His voice was kind but did not allow room for further debate. Reluctantly the two children turned and left the room.

Mary gave a sigh of relief. "I'm sorry, Jamie. We usually lock the door before we begin the therapy."

Jamie ignored her and turned his stone-gray eyes toward the nurse. 'How would you say she's progressing, Mrs. Wright?"

Jan gave him an encouraging smile. "Very well indeed, Mr. Fitzhugh. Why, another week, and the bandages will be off entirely."

With an effort he forced himself to look at Mary's hands again, and Mary thought she saw him shudder. "The scars will fade, won't they?"

Jan's smile faltered. "Well, of course, in time the redness will fade, but ..."

Anger surged through Mary. How dare they talk about her as though she were not there? His distaste at the sight of her injuries was obvious, so why didn't he just go instead of continuing to stare at her hands so oddly? "What do you suggest," she muttered through clenched teeth, still not free of the pain, "plastic surgery to make them pretty?"

He took no note of her sarcasm. "If need be," he pronounced emphatically.

She sneered. "Well, you'll pardon me if I'm more interested in getting back the use of these hands than I am in winning beauty contests with them."

He looked at her in surprise. "Well, of course you'll get full use back." He stared at her through narrowed lids, and something in the scornful look she returned made him turn to Jan for reassurance. "Won't she?"

Jan shrugged. "That's what we're hoping for — what we're working for — and the doctor is becoming more optimistic each day, but —"

"No one said anything to me about impaired use, or anything less than a complete recovery," he thundered, as though he would have forbidden such a turn of events if it had been suggested. He rose abruptly, and it seemed to Mary that he could not bear to be in the same room with the hands that would never be aesthetically pleasing again. "Damn it, get on with the therapy, then, and see that you do a good job of it, Mrs. Wright, or you'll answer to me. And so will that idiot doctor." He strode over to the door, where he stopped and turned back to look at the slight figure on the bed who was still reeling from his unexplained anger. "Damn you, Manya!" He slammed the door as an exclamation point and was gone.

"Well! What was that all about?" Jan asked curiously, and when Mary did not answer, she lifted one of the injured hands and began to exercise it again. This time Mary was hardly aware of what she was doing, her thoughts still trying to digest Jamie's strange behavior.

Jamie had avoided her all week, and at this, their first meeting, he had been furious because she had frightened the children, and repelled at the sight of her swollen and deformed hands. She looked down at them as Jan continued to work the stiff fingers smoothly between her own efficient hands. It was true they were ugly, but at least they were moving and would soon be capable of performing useful functions.

Perhaps he thought that the extent of her injuries would result in his being saddled with her for additional months while she underwent plastic surgery to improve their appearance. Well, he needn't worry on that score. Once she had the use of her hands again, there was no way she would consider invaliding herself for any further length of time merely to improve their cosmetic appearance.

"Whatever is that frown for?" Jan observed. "I know I'm hurting you, but this is the first time you've looked like you would like to murder me for it."

Mary forced a smile and uttered some inane excuse and then turned all her concentration on the exercises they were doing. When they were finished, Jan gave her a triumphant smile.

"You're coming along so well, I've decided you deserve a treat."

Mary looked at her without enthusiasm. No doubt she was to be rewarded with a special dessert—one she could not even eat without help, she thought resentfully. However, Jan surprised her.

"How would you like to take a shower?" Jan's suggestion was based on a fine knowledge of her patient's likes and dislikes; and she knew that the ritual bed baths rated high on Mary's list of dislikes.

Mary stared at her. "You're joking. What about the bandages?"

"I won't redo them until after you've had that shower. Of course, I'll still have to come with you to wash you, but it will be so much more refreshing in the shower, and we can even give that heavy mane of yours a proper shampoo. It will be much more comfortable than our previous efforts leaning over the bathroom sink."

She was so anxious to please that Mary was ashamed of herself. "Oh, Jan, I have been a grouch, haven't I? A shower sounds great, and you're a dear to suggest it." Mary's eyes sparkled in anticipation, causing Jan to be very pleased with herself. There seemed to be little enough in this strange household to make her patient's eyes light up.

Carefully she helped Mary off the bed and supported her into the large bathroom, where she helped her remove her nightgown before leading her into the glass-enclosed shower, where a tall step stool had been strategically placed.

"I didn't think you would be strong enough to stand for long this first time," Jan explained as she helped Mary to sit on the stool.

Mary gave her an impish look. "Are you planning to come into the shower with me, dressed like that?" Her eyes gleamed mischievously as she took in Jan's starched white uniform.

The two women looked at each other and exploded with laughter. "Well," Jan joked when she caught her breath, "I thought about the stool, but I forgot about the fool. Be patient while I run down to my room and slip into my bathing suit and get a terry cloth robe. I'll just be a moment. You won't fall or anything, if I leave you?" she worried.

Mary gave a light laugh. "I'll be fine. In fact, turn on the water before you leave. I'll enjoy having it splash down on me while I wait."

Jan bent into the shower stall and adjusted the water until it was neither too hot, nor too cold, stepping back as far as she could from the expected spray as a gentle cascade of warm water fell on her patient. "Now, don't you move from that spot until I return," she cautioned and closed the glass shower door behind her as she hurried away.

The water felt heavenly, and Mary perched on the stool, luxuriating in the sensuous feel of it on her soft skin. Pleased with herself at the moment, she began to hum a tuneless ditty.

It seemed only minutes later when she heard the bathroom door open again. "That was fast," she called out over the sound of the water through the glass door. "You must have run all the way."

There was no answer, but she saw the rippled shadow of a figure dropping a robe to the floor. Strange, she thought absently, how the glass distorted Jan's figure and made her seem so much larger. And then the shower door was pulled open, and she saw that it was not a distortion at all.

"Hello, sweetheart," her husband's sardonic voice greeted her as he stepped naked into the shower to join her.

"Are you out of your mind?" she gasped. "Get out of here before Jan comes back."

"Jan won't be coming back for a while. I told her I would see to your shower. Since I was about to have one of my own, anyway, there was no reason for her to get wet." Mary was suffocatingly conscious of his huge, sinewy body filling the small shower cubicle and dominating it with his masculinity.

"You—you can't do this!"

"Of course I can. I'm here, aren't I?" He purposely misunderstood her. "It's not as though I haven't helped you to shower before."

"But I don't want you here . . . like this . . . with

me," she mumbled, trying weakly to rise. His heavy hand on her shoulder held her firmly down on the stool.

"Don't worry, sweetheart. You're not about to be attacked. Just washed," he mocked.

The scornful sound of the word *sweetheart* on his lips sounded like an obscenity and was another indication that he was intent upon humiliating and punishing her, taking a perverse pleasure in having trapped her naked and helpless in the steaming shower.

"This is indecent," she objected as he took a bar of soap and ran it with deliberate slowness over her shoulders and down her arms, rubbing the lather into her skin with long strokes of his sensitive fingertips. Then his soapy hands worked their way down her back in tantalizing circular motions that left her skin tingling even as the roving fingers moved on downward to finally rest on her hips in a possessive gesture. His hands probed deeply, slowly, not unaware of the sensations he was bringing to life as he traced soapy patterns over a terrain that was well known to him. In spite of herself, she trembled and bit her lips to stifle a moan that was half protest, half pleasure.

"I'm not hurting you, am I, sweetheart?" The husky throb in his voice made it all too apparent that he knew exactly what she was feeling.

Jamie was kneeling beside the stool now, one arm wound around her waist, fingers splayed against her stomach for support, oblivious of the water that was pouring over his own head and shoulders as he washed the lather off her back with gentle strokes of his other hand. When Mary thought she could not bear the sweet agony of his touch another second, he rose abruptly to stand behind her. From the sounds she heard she knew that he was washing himself.

"This is almost like old times, isn't it, sweetheart?" he chortled with false bravado. "Except, of course, that now it would be your turn to wash me. Ah, well, when your hands are completely well, we can work on that." To her surprise he burst into song—a risqué sea shanty from his navy days that she had heard often in the past.

"If you think that I would ever again . . . willingly . . ." She broke off without finishing the sentence. She would not dignify his suggestion by even discussing it. "Are you quite through?" she asked through stiff lips.

In answer, his hands came down to twist themselves in the long, wet strands of her hair. "Hardly." He disabused her of that notion quickly. "Next, but not last, this enticing mane gets shampooed. Lean back against me, tip your head up, and close your eyes so that you won't get soap in them."

Mary sat there stiffly and made no move to obey. With an indulgent laugh at her futile defiance, he maneuvered her into the desired position until the back of her head rested against the flat, muscled planes of his stomach. Then, reaching for the shampoo on the shelf, he proceeded to lather her long blond hair, his fingers digging deeply into her scalp, massaging it until it tingled.

"Mmmm, that feels good," she murmured before she could stop herself, and then, horrified at her own stupidity, she clamped her lips together.

Jamie gave an exultant laugh. "You always were a sucker for having your head rubbed." His fingers continued their hypnotic magic on her scalp, and she suffered the soothing motions with a heavy sigh that she hoped he would take as resignation rather than contentment.

"By the way, you really needed this," his voice droned on over the sound of the falling water. "Your hair was filthy. I thought it looked much darker than I remembered it. Now, when it dries, it should be the color of cornsilk again."

She wanted to ask if he had any idea of how difficult it was to wash hair as long as hers in a bathroom basin under the best of circumstances, much less when her injuries made it difficult to maneuver, but his proximity was interfering with her simplest thought processes.

Mary clenched her lips to stifle a groan as he moved to one side of her and slipped a hand firmly under her neck to support her as he bent her slowly back until her hair fell freely down her back into the path of the cascading water. The fingers of his other hand slid through her hair, separating the strands, exposing them to the spray, which rinsed the shampoo away.

"Beautiful," he murmured, his anger seemingly sliding down the drain with the last of the soapy water.

She sighed again, forgetting for the moment everything but the warm memories he had unlocked from the past. In an almost dreamlike state she became aware that he had taken his hands out of her hair and was moving around to stand in front of her. Her eyes could not see beyond the wide, muscular expanse of chest and shoulders that seemed to fill the small shower stall, her gaze riveted to the mass of sandy curls that were now matted wetly down on his chest, and beyond, making her shockingly aware of his body.

Unable to stop themselves, her eyes continued their exploration down past his narrow hips to the sinewy length of his thighs. She had forgotten how hairy his legs were, but suddenly she was flooded with the memory of how the feel of his hirsute roughness against her own smooth skin had always inflamed her senses.

This was madness, she groaned inwardly, wrenching her eyes away in confused embarrassment. Even if they had both been fully clothed, the shower stall was much too small to contain them; naked, she felt herself succumbing to the traitorous pull of her senses and the capricious whims of his overwhelming masculinity. "I want to get out of here," she begged piteously.

His eyes glittered. "Not yet, sweetheart. I haven't finished with you." He slid down on one knee in front of her and reached again for the bar of soap, lathering it in his hands. Then he transferred the fragrant suds to her upper body, just above the swell of her breasts. Then, slowly, using both hands, he rubbed the lather into her skin.

"Please, don't," she whimpered.

"Oh, yes, sweetheart," he muttered thickly,

"oh yes." Mary closed her eyes in resignation, but it only seemed to intensify the sensations caused by his hands roaming over her breasts, his thumbs circling her nipples, coaxing them to rise up traitorously to welcome his touch. She bit her lip to keep from crying out for the touch of his mouth again.

It had been so long, so long, since his hands had claimed her so. She swayed, almost in a faint, and his strong hands reached up and placed her arms on his shoulders for balance. Her head dipped in mute surrender, her forehead coming to rest against the top of his bent head.

Assuring himself that she was balanced and would not fall, his hands were busy again, running down each of her legs, soaping them, rinsing them, caressing them. Her body sagged further against him and he quickly raised his face to look up at her. Her eyes were closed; her lower lip, bruised from where she had bitten it, was waiting to be kissed.

She looked beautiful, vulnerable, wanton, and yet... God, it would be so easy to lose himself once again in that beauty; to forget the past and remember only that the woman in his arms was his wife, the woman he loved. *No*. Damn it, she was the woman he had *once* loved. She meant nothing to him now. Why the hell had he started this farce?

The desire in his eyes hardened to anger and self-revulsion as he refused to be drawn into her spell. One blunt-tipped finger reached up to cup an aroused breast, squeezing it until she opened her eyes. "You've lost weight," he observed insolently as his fingers weighed her breast.

"Why are you doing this to me?" Tears of humiliation filled her bright aquamarine eyes, enraging him.

Because I can't help myself, he groaned inwardly.

"Because I was curious to see if I could still excite you," he said aloud. "Stupid of me, wasn't it, since obviously any man can do that. You were always easy." He had to be cruel to keep himself from succumbing to the pull of his overwhelming need for her. He was just a breath away from surrendering his pride and his self-respect.

The unfairness of his accusation jerked her head back as forcefully as if he had struck her. The longing to have him take her into his arms and make love to her was instantly replaced by fury and remembered hatred. "Well, you've had enough easy women to know, haven't you?" she countered.

Jamie raised his hand as if to slap her, hesitated a moment, and then reached over to turn the faucet full force on cold. "We could both use a cold shower," he commented wryly and proceeded to freeze them both under the icy water before he relented and turned the tap off completely.

With the shower turned off, they could hear Jan tapping frantically on the locked bathroom door. "Is everything all right in there?"

Without hurrying, Jamie stepped out of the shower and into his robe, roughly rubbing his hair dry with a nearby towel. Then, reaching for the large bath sheet that was hanging on the wall, he wrapped it around Mary's shivering shoulders, lifting her, with the same motion, off the stool and into his arms.

Reaching down awkwardly, he unlocked the bathroom door and pushed it open with his hip, carrying Mary into the bedroom. "Here's your patient, Mrs. Wright, all squeaky clean and ready for bed. Too bad I can't join her there"—he smiled teasingly for the nurse's benefit—"but duty calls. But we'll do this again, won't we, sweetheart?"

To Mary, held fast in his arms, the derision in his voice made her oblivious to the shuttered pain in his eyes. She shivered again at his confident attitude, which said more plainly than words that if and when he desired to join her in bed, there was no way she would be able to stop him. And she knew it was true. No matter how many times she told herself that she hated him, as far as he was concerned she would always be "easy."

Chapter Six

"Ma'am?" Cal poked his head into the opened sitting room door. The drapes were drawn, and in the dim light it was not clear if anyone was there, yet he knew his mother never left this room.

A voice drifted faintly out to him from the darkest corner. "I'm not feeling very well, Cal. Why don't you run along and play."

He stood uncertainly in the doorway, trying to peer through the darkness. "I don't have anyone to play with. Jaycie has gone out with her mother, and Bill's gone to the dentist." Bill was a friend down the street who attended the same private school that Cal did.

"Well, why don't you go into the family room and watch TV," suggested the tear-muffled voice from the darkened room.

"Can I watch in here with you, ma'am?"

"Not if you keep calling me ma'am," she snapped wretchedly. From her chair she saw his small shoulders slump as he turned to leave. Instantly she regretted the sharp way she had spoken to him. What was wrong with her that she should be taking her misery out on Cal? Jamie's little performance this morning must have unnerved her more than she realized.

"Cal," she called out to the retreating figure. "Come back...please. Actually, I'm alone, too. Jan has gone to the store, and I have just been sitting here brooding."

"What's brooding?" He hurried into the room before she could change her mind. "Does it mean sitting in the dark?"

She managed a trace of a smile. "Well, it sort of means thinking about unpleasant things and wishing they were different. But sitting in the dark does seem to encourage it. Why don't you open the drapes, and I'm sure my gloomy thoughts will all fly away."

Anxious to be of service, he stumbled over his own feet as he drew open the draperies. Then, instead of going over to turn on the TV, he walked up to her chair and stared at her. "Your eyes are all red," he observed with a worried frown. "Did Mrs. Wright hurt you again?"

"Mrs. Wright is very good to me," she hastened to allay his fears. "Your dad was right. If she does hurt me, it's only to make me better. You mustn't think harshly of her."

He continued to stare at her with troubled eyes. "What *should* I call you?"

When she gave him an uncomprehending look, he went on to explain. "You were angry because I called you ma'am."

"Why *do* you call me that?" She kept her voice carefully neutral. "Was it your dad's idea?"

"N-no. Dad said I could call you whatever I wanted," he hastened to explain, "but Barbara said that since you wouldn't be staying very long, that I shouldn't get too familiar. She said ma'am was polite and would suit you fine."

Barbara again. Would that woman never stop interfering in her life!

"I brooded about that a lot," he confessed, his gray eyes searching her face for an answer. "If—if you were going to s-stay," he continued eagerly, "then m-maybe I c-could call you m-m...you know," he finished lamely.

Mary's arms ached to gather him close and wipe the confused, self-conscious look off his face. Didn't he know how much she wanted just what he wanted? But, of course, she could not stay. Jamie had made it very clear that she could never hope to have a permanent place in her son's life. As soon as his political future was settled, she would be sent packing. There was no assurance she could give the boy that would not be based on lies, and she would not do that.

"You mustn't brood, Cal," she soothed. "I'm here now, and we can be good friends for . . . for as long as I stay."

Without a word he walked away from her and turned on the TV. She could tell by the dull look in his eyes and the trembling set of his mouth that her answer had destroyed him.

"But you could call me Mother anyway. If you wanted to," she ended lamely.

He busied himself switching stations on the TV.

"I guess not, if you're really not going to stay." He refused to look at her.

"I would stay, if I could," she assured him, but when he turned to look at her with hope-filled eyes, she added firmly, "but I can't!"

He gave an indifferent shrug of his shoulders, but the slight wobble of his chin betrayed him. "That's what Barbara said." He gave his full attention to the flickering TV screen.

His acceptance of Barbara's word as law infuriated her. Maybe she could not fight Jamie, but Barbara was another matter. "Shut off that TV," she commanded, "and we'll talk about this." This was one round that Barbara would not win without a fight.

He turned toward her with his lips set in a stubborn line, ready to defy her, but something in the equally stubborn set of her own jaw dissuaded him. He switched off the TV and went over to sit on the stool by her side, waiting with skeptical eyes for her to speak.

"I know you're angry because I left you when you were a baby," she began, "and you have a right to be. I was wrong and I'm sorry. My only excuse is that I only expected to be gone a few days; and later, when I realized that I couldn't come back after all, I knew that your dad would never allow you to live with me. You see, I had no money, and you would have had to stay with a sitter while I was away at work."

"We could have both lived with Dad," he accused. "Dad has lots of money."

"No," she contradicted. "I couldn't come back. You have to believe that and try to understand the rest. Your dad and I both loved you very much, but you could only live with one of us."

"I'll never leave Dad," he interrupted quickly, frightened at the direction her words seemed to be leading.

She tried to reassure him. "I know. And I would never ask you to do that. Your place is with your father. I knew that all those years ago when I first left you, and I haven't changed my mind about it. He can give you the whole world, and I want you to have it."

Mary paused to take a deep breath. "But, now that you're getting to be such a big boy, I thought maybe we could at least be real friends and keep on being friends even when I don't live here anymore."

"You'll go away and I'll never see you again," he blurted out.

"No, honey, no," she promised. "That's what I'm trying to explain. It's true that I won't always be living in the same house with you, but I won't really be going away. I'll live somewhere nearby so that we can visit each other, and maybe you can even write me letters, and I'll write back to you."

"I don't write yet." He sighed hopelessly. "Just my name and address."

She refused to be discouraged; at least he was still listening to her. "But you will be writing soon, and as you get older, it will be easy for you. In the meantime, we could call each other up and talk on the telephone."

"What would we talk about?" He pouted.

She laughed excitedly. "Everything! The books you're learning to read, the TV shows you're watching, what new mischief Jaycie has gotten herself into, what you had for dinner. Oh, we'd have lots and lots to talk about...if we were friends."

"You left me," he remembered darkly. "I was a baby and you left me. So why would you want to be friends now?"

"Because I'm sorry for what I did...and because I love you."

"If you were really sorry, you wouldn't ever go away again," he reasoned stubbornly. He was truly his father's son.

She sighed in defeat. Seven years old, no matter how bright, was still a child. In his simplistic world a mother who loved him would never leave him.

"Well, I *am* going away," she admitted flatly, "and there's no use pretending I'm not. But not right away," she added quickly, hoping to erase the mutinous pout that was clouding his features. "And not very far away. Can we at least be friends for the time I'm here? I'll be here for a long time yet," she promised, "at least until after Christmas."

"Christmas!" He gave an incredulous sigh of relief. "Why, that's forever away. It isn't even summer yet."

She took heart again. "Yes, we'll have all summer to spend together—Fourth of July, Halloween, Thanksgiving, and then Christmas." She translated time into something he could relate to easily. "And soon I'll be well enough so that we can go out together and do all sorts of fun things. But I won't enjoy being here at all if you aren't my friend," she added truthfully.

Mary could see Cal struggling with himself. She was not offering what he wanted, but she was offering something. He jumped to his feet and stuck out his hand for her to shake, and then ruefully brought it back to his side.

"Okay. We'll be friends until after Christmas. But I don't know about after that, m-ma'am."

"But you'll have to forget that stuffy ma'am," she insisted, coming back to the point of their original discussion. "I know. You can call me Manya. My mother used to call me that when I was your age. But no one calls me that anymore." A shadow crossed her face, but she smiled it away. "It would be a special name just between the two of us."

"Manya." He savored the sound. "It sounds like..." His face reddened, but he pushed on boldly. "It sounds like mother."

Her heart ached for what she was denying him. "It's a Polish word that means Mary," she corrected gently, "but it could have a special meaning just for us, if you like."

"Manya," he agreed happily. And then, with the single-mindedness of a child, he closed the subject. "Can we watch cartoons now?"

With a laugh she agreed, and they spent the rest of the hour giggling at the antics of Road Runner. When the program ended, he turned back to Mary with a diffident expression on his face.

"Can I stay and have supper with you? Dad

won't be home until late," he continued hurriedly, "and it's not fun eating in the big dining room
by myself."

She hesitated. Mealtimes were the worst part of
the day for her, and she balked at having Cal see
how helpless she was then, unable even to feed
herself.

He sensed her hesitation. "I could help Mrs.
Wright take care of you, Manya," he appealed;
and the tender way he said her name melted her
resistance.

"Okay, Cal," she agreed with some misgivings.
"Jan is probably in the kitchen right now getting a
tray ready. Why don't you ask her to make one up
for you, too?"

Actually, it was not as awkward as she had
imagined it would be. Cal ate his own dinner with
gusto; and, sensing her embarrassment, he hardly
looked in her direction as Jan carefully cut her
meat and fed her with her usual brisk efficiency.
The three of them laughed throughout most of
the meal as Cal told hoary riddles that the two
women pretended they had never heard before.

"Tell me"—Mary giggled helplessly—"where
does a five-hundred-pound gorilla sit?" And at his
serious delivery of the anticipated punch line,
tears of mirth ran down her cheeks and she dou-
bled over in genuine laughter.

At that moment the tall, forbidding presence of
her husband stood silhouetted in the doorframe,
an angry, puzzled look on his grim face.

"I wondered where you were, Cal." His tight
voice asked a question.

Cal was still giggling proudly over the effects of

his riddle on his rapt audience. "I didn't expect you home, Dad," he said in easy explanation, "so I thought I would keep Manya company."

"Manya?" The dark look on his face deepened into a scowl.

"She said I could call her that." Cal looked from his mother to his father uncertainly. "It's a Polish word that means Mary." He shared his new knowledge proudly. "That's what they used to call her when she was little, and now it's my special name for her," he finished lamely, aware that he had somehow incurred his father's further displeasure. "It's all right, isn't it, Dad?"

Jamie did not answer. His gray eyes were busily roaming the room, assessing the scene before him. The dishes on his son's dinner tray were all wiped clean, except for a neat pile of buttered carrots that had been put to one side of his plate. Jamie's eyes riveted on the carrots and then moved questioningly back to his son, who hurriedly picked up his fork.

"I—I told him he didn't have to finish them if he didn't like them." Mary had followed his censoring glance and the almost imperceptible signal to their son. Her foolish comment had the unpleasant effect of drawing those stern eyes to her own tray, which still contained a great deal of uneaten food, despite Jan's best efforts.

"Perhaps you should set him a better example," he suggested in wintry disapproval. Their eyes locked in battle.

Defiantly she turned to Jan. "You can take my tray back to the kitchen now. I've had enough."

Jan, traitor that she was, looked questioningly at Jamie. He gave a curt nod, and gratefully she picked up the tray and fairly flew out of the room; but Mary was not unaware that she would not have left without Jamie's permission. She looked over at Cal, who was chewing his carrots with a martyred air, and then back at her husband. "You're really quite a bully, do you know that?"

He gave a snort that was meant to pass as laughter, and then surprised her by sinking into an easy chair and crossing his long legs in a lazy gesture that made it evident that he was not in a hurry to leave. "I've got a new knock-knock joke for you, Cal." He had turned slightly in the chair so that his back was to Mary and he devoted his attention totally to his son.

She accepted the snub with a slight thinning of her lips and sat back quietly, watching as he deliberately charmed her son's attention away from her. It was obvious that he had seated himself in her sitting room for the sole purpose of proving to her that she could not take his place in Cal's affections.

As though she would even try.

Today was the first time she had ever broken through her son's reserve completely, and sensing this, Jamie seemed determined to take even that small victory away from her.

The carrots finished, Cal was perched on his father's knee now, and the two of them rattled off familiar knock-knock jokes to each other while Mary sat behind them, apparently forgotten. A surge of self-pity engulfed her and traitorous tears welled in her eyes. She moved quickly to wipe them away with the back of her bandaged hands. Her movements, though furtive, called attention to her, and Jamie turned slowly in the chair, his arm still resting possessively on his son's shoulder, to look in her direction.

Thankfully the tears had been erased, and she stared back at him with expressionless eyes. The two of them stared at each other, and though she flinched inwardly at the hate she saw reflected there, she refused to give him the satisfaction of looking away. *It's my hands that have been injured, not my backbone,* her defiant expression shouted.

"Do you know any knock-knock jokes, Manya?" Cal's bright voice broke through the tenseness.

She looked past his father to smile at him. "I'm afraid not," she admitted in a small voice.

"Off to bed, Son," Jamie broke in. "I want to talk to...er...Manya." He kissed the top of Cal's head. "Bring the tray down to the kitchen and then be sure to stop in to say good night to Grandpa Fitz, and remember to take a bath. I'll be in to say good night later."

"Okay, Dad." He scampered off his father's lap and started to leave the room. At the door he hesitated, looking back at Mary, who gave him a small wave of her bandaged hand in farewell. With a quick grin he raced back into the room and gave her a moist peck on the cheek. "It's been fun having both you and Dad to myself," he confessed. "Good night."

The heaviness that had engulfed her disappeared at the featherlight brush of his lips on her cheek. He had enjoyed being with her as well as Jamie. She clutched that thought fiercely to her, sighing deeply without being aware that she had done so.

"So you've made a conquest of him, Manya." The sardonic voice lingered silkily over her name. "It didn't take you too long, did it? Three weeks and he's eating out of your hand."

"I thought you wanted us to be friends."

"That depends." His voice was accusing. "What promises did you make to him that you can't keep?"

"I told him I would be here until Christmas." She strove to keep her voice calm. "You know better than I if that's a promise I can keep."

"And after that?" he prodded.

"And after that I told him I planned to live in the area close by so that we could talk to each other on the phone and perhaps see each other occasionally. With your permission." She faltered over the last, admitting her vulnerability.

"I would set certain conditions on such visits, of course." His light eyes glittered like melting icicles.

"Oh?"

"I would never allow him to see you while you were living with your lover," he said bluntly.

Her face blanched at the insult, but she struggled to retain her composure, knowing she would gain nothing by arguing with him. "I have no lover," she protested.

He dismissed her protest with unbelieving eyes.

"Good. Then there's no problem, is there? But if he should return..." He allowed his sentence to dangle ominously. "Just don't expect to have your cake and eat it, too."

Anger burned in her throat as she thought of him living openly in this house with Barbara and Jaycie and Cal. He dared to deny her access to her son if she should have a lover, yet he obviously had no qualms about exposing Cal to Barbara and their illegitimate child.

As though reading her mind, he smiled unpleasantly. "Oh, about our plans to move into the Mission Hills house. I've changed my mind. It would be ridiculous to reopen that house for only eight months, especially as you and I will be away campaigning a good deal of that time, and Cal would have to stay here anyway while we were away."

She gasped in disbelief. "You promised," she accused.

Again the icicle glitter of those expressive gray eyes. "I lied," he said flatly. "Politicians are notorious for doing that, aren't they?"

"I won't stay on in this house," she fumed. "I'll leave as soon as I'm well."

"That should be soon, according to the good doctor," he informed her cruelly. "I had a long talk with him today. Your bandages will come off this week, and a week of exercise and walking around should bring you up to speed. In spite of the misgivings you and Mrs. Wright were laboring under, it seems you are making remarkable progress," he added mockingly.

"Then I'll soon leave." She repeated her threat.

"Oh?" He obviously relished being thoroughly in control of the situation. "I thought I understood you to say that you told Cal you would be here until after Christmas. You've changed your mind, then?"

She bit her lip in vexation. "I thought we would be moving to our own home."

The smile left his face. "*We* have no *home*. And, as a place to live, this house is as good as any other. It's familiar to Cal; and as you and I will be away campaigning quite a bit, he'll be happier here among people he knows—like his grandfather."

"And Barbara, of course," she said with unconcealed bitterness, "and her daughter."

"Yes," he agreed smoothly. "Cal and Jaycie are good company for each other."

His casual acceptance of the situation grated on her nerves. Didn't he realize that she knew all about Barbara...about Jaycie? Of course he did, but he was so arrogant that he did not care. He enjoyed humiliating her by forcing her to live in the shadow of his mistress and their child.

"I hate you," she said quietly, her voice thick with anger at the trap he was closing about her.

A dark shadow flickered in his eyes as he gave a bitter laugh. "If your hate is as constant as your love, I'm sure you'll soon be over it. In the meantime, sweetheart, may I assume that you have decided to stay on with us until after Christmas?"

Mary longed to scratch that insolent, infuriating smile off his face, and she promised herself it would be one of the first things she did when she regained the use of her hands. Now the memory of Cal, of the eager, expectant look in his eyes as they had discussed the months together that loomed ahead of them, made her hesitate. The door of the trap swung tightly shut, and she bent her head in defeat.

"You know I'll stay."

Chapter Seven

An uneasy truce settled over the house. The morning therapy sessions had finally come to an end as Mary gradually regained the use of her fingers. When she was able to feed herself, Jamie insisted that she have her meals in the dining room with him, Cal, and Fitz—a situation she had been dreading. Her manual dexterity still left a lot to be desired and she did not relish the thought of being on display as she laboriously forced her fingers to assume the responsibility for getting a fork or a spoon to her lips without spilling the contents onto the table or her clothing. However, being coerced into doing so certainly speeded the recovery process since, under Jamie's critical eye, she could not bear to fail when doing so would earn her his contempt or, worse still, his pity.

At first her stiff fingers curled around the eating utensils the way Cal's had when he was a baby, but eventually they relearned the proper responses; and though the end result was still far from graceful, it no longer required the same fierce concentration it had initially to get through an entire meal without disgracing herself.

To her immense relief she was spared the additional indignity of having Barbara witness her pitifully slow progress, since Barbara and Jaycie did not take their meals with the family but ate separately with Jan. Fitz, it seemed, had developed an intense dislike for his former mistress—brought on, Mary assumed, by the fact that Barbara had betrayed him with his son—and while he allowed her to stay on in the household as a servant, he refused to give her or her daughter any social status or to tolerate their presence in the same room with him, unless absolutely necessary to the running of the household.

Whatever his reason, this attitude on his part also spared Mary the agony of having to observe her husband and his mistress, and their child, as a family, and for this, too, she was intensely grateful.

Jaycie, without Barbara's presence to remind Mary that this was her husband's illegitimate child, was another matter. Mary could not help but respond to the child's undemanding, affectionate nature. When Cal came to visit Mary, Jaycie was inevitably with him, and it would not be too long before Jaycie found her way into Mary's lap, where she would watch silently, thumb in her mouth, as Mary and Cal played card games. Sometimes the children would draw pictures for Mary's approval, and after a while, Jan would arrive on the scene with the tray of milk and cookies that had become an afternoon ritual with them.

Sometimes Fitz would come home early from

the office to visit with his grandson, and since he was usually to be found in Mary's suite of rooms, he would huff and puff his way down the hallway to join them and quite often made a willing partner in a game of three-handed rummy or pinochle.

Jaycie seemed genuinely fond of the older man, despite Fitz making no secret of the fact that her childish attentions annoyed him. More than once he made a point of calling for Barbara and asking her to remove the child from his presence and, white-faced and grim, but without comment, the housekeeper would take her daughter into her arms and carry her out of the room. Young as she was, Jaycie made no complaint; she had already learned that Mr. Fitz was to be obeyed without fail.

At such times Fitz would look questioningly at Mary, waiting for her comment but she refused to give him the satisfaction of rising to the bait. It was obvious that he knew that Jaycie was his son's child; and while he tolerated her presence in his house, he refused to acknowledge that she had any familial status.

"Do you object?" he questioned Mary sharply on one such occasion when he had dismissed Jaycie from the room. Mary said nothing. "I should think you would approve heartily that I favor Cal as my only heir." His shrewd eyes searched hers for a reaction.

"Cal doesn't need your money," she forced herself to remind him in a disinterested manner. "His father is not exactly a pauper."

"Perhaps," Fitz admitted, "but already his father has diluted the boy's inheritance by providing for another." He gave Mary another sharp glance. "That doesn't bother you?"

"It doesn't concern me," she snapped more bitterly than she intended, and was immediately angry with herself for even betraying to Fitz that she knew about the trust fund that Jamie had established for Jaycie.

"You and Barbara used to be friends," he commented, "but that's no longer true, is it? That leads me to believe that you're not a complete fool, after all. Surely you realize that Barbara is very ambitious for that child of hers. She would do anything to have the girl acknowledged as a Fitzhugh; and failing that, she will try to get as much money out of us as she can. I'm on to her greedy little schemes, but Jamie feels the family has a responsibility toward her, so you'll have to watch out for her in that corner."

"What Jamie does is of no concern to me," she replied with more conviction than she felt. "Cal is all I care about."

"Then I was wrong. You *are* a fool," he retorted, "and I see that I will have to continue to look out for your interests as well as my grandson's."

His comment angered Mary into goading, "If you don't like having Barbara around, why do you keep her on?"

The older man grimaced. "Surely you've guessed that Jamie has given me an ultimatum. If I send Barbara away without making a heavy settlement on her and the child, Jamie will have nothing more to do with me. And since I refuse to make that greedy woman rich at our expense, we're at a stalemate. I had hoped that your coming here would divert Jamie's attention to other areas, but you've let me down, Miss Mary." He heaved a heavy sigh and rose from the chair, leaving her alone with her thoughts.

This bit of information explained many things that had been puzzling her. Now she understood why Jamie had refused to reopen their old house. Only his continued presence in this house kept Fitz from ridding himself of both Barbara and Jaycie and the threat they constituted to the Fitzhugh name. Fitz had obviously been hoping that Jamie would be so engrossed in his legal family that he would forget about his mistress and her demands, but it hadn't worked out that way. Jamie was obviously even more bewitched by Barbara and Jaycie than Fitz realized.

Establishing the trust fund for Jaycie had been only the first step. Mary had no doubt that Barbara would soon succeed in getting him to establish an independent income for her as well. Her ultimate goal, of course, was to have Jamie formally acknowledge Jaycie as his daughter to the world. However, in view of his political aspirations, she might have a difficult time on that score. Illegitimate children, no matter how charming, did not rate very highly with the voters, which explained Mary's own presence here. The fact that she was living in the same house with Barbara and Jaycie reduced the chances that any inquiring reporter would discover the true state of musical bedrooms that existed in the outwardly respectable Fitzhugh mansion.

Despite her misery at Jamie's perfidy, the thought came to Mary that perhaps she could use the threat of revealing his relationship with Barbara as leverage for getting more liberal visitation rights with Cal after she left this house.

She was mulling this possibility over in her mind when she noticed that Jaycie had crept back into the room and was looking around with anxious eyes. "I saw Mr. Fitz leave. Can I come in and sit with you again? Mummy's having a headache and I can't find Cal anywhere. I think he's gone out to play with the big kids."

Mary nodded her head in assent, and Jaycie scrambled into her lap, snuggling comfortably against her shoulder. "Why doesn't Mr. Fitz like me?" she asked in bewilderment. "He likes Cal, and I try to behave just as gooder as Cal does."

Mary wrapped her arms comfortingly around the small child and rocked her slowly back and forth. "Don't you worry about grumpy old Fitz. I think you're very, very nice," she consoled.

"And so do I," a deep, teasing voice added from somewhere behind them. "That's why I've brought you a present."

"Jamie?" Jaycie clapped her hands and wiggled out of Mary's lap. "A present for me? I love presents!"

"That's because you're a female," he observed dryly as he handed her a small, fluffy stuffed teddy bear. "Your mother told me you were afraid of the dark, so I brought you a friend to keep you company in bed."

Mary bit her lip. No one could accuse him of not being a good father. This gesture was typical of the tender, thoughtful manner with which he treated both of his children. Jaycie's face was pressed against his cheek, emphasizing the similarity in their skin and hair tones. Dismayed at the sense of loss that surged through her because this child of his was not her child as well, she turned her face away.

Jamie swung the girl up on one hip and whispered something into her ear. Jaycie looked at Mary and giggled. With an answering laugh, he set her on her feet and gave her a playful slap on the rump to head her out of the room.

"You look good with Jaycie in your arms," he said unevenly as he sank into the chair that Fitz had just recently vacated. Confused and embarrassed, she started to rise. Their truce did not extend to the point where they could be natural in each other's presence without the buffer of one or the other of the children present.

"Don't go." He put out a hand to stop her, and her skin burned under his touch. She tugged lightly to free her wrist from his grasp. "Don't go," he repeated, but this time the uncertainty had left his voice, and it was a command. She sat back in her chair and folded her hands in her lap in a resigned gesture.

"You look like a schoolgirl about to get bawled out by the principal," he observed with a wry smile.

"And am I? About to get bawled out?" she taunted. She hated him for the effect just being near him had on her nervous system. She hated him for being Jaycie's father. There was no way she could be relaxed and act naturally when she found herself alone with him.

"You don't make it easy for either of us, do you know that?" He gave a weary sigh. "We'll never make it to Christmas at this rate. If we can't be friends, can't we at least be polite to each other?"

"Of course," she agreed in what she hoped was a polite enough manner to suit him, but she looked pointedly down at the red mark on her wrist where he had grabbed her. "That, I presume, is your idea of polite?"

With an angry imprecation he sank back in a chair. "You never let up, do you?"

"Did you want me for any special reason, or were you just looking for a sparring partner?"

"Mary, if you say another word to me in that prissy voice, I swear I'll turn you over my knee and whip you the way I would Cal. And believe me, he's never given me as much provocation as you have!"

Wisely she said nothing, merely refolded her hands in her lap and waited.

"I'm letting Jan go," he said abruptly, and at the horrified expression on Mary's face, he continued quickly, "You don't need her any longer. You're much better and there simply isn't enough useful work for her to do here. I've made arrangements for her to take a vacation for a few weeks, and after that she has another case lined up where she will really be needed.''

''How dare you! Jan isn't just my nurse. She's my friend—the only friend I have in this tomb of a house! You're just being mean because you know how much her company means to me.''

''That's not so.'' Jamie's voice was unexpectedly gentle, as though he understood her anguish at this unexpected turn of events. ''Actually, it was Jan's idea. You're becoming too dependent upon her—letting her run interference for you, while you retreat into some dreamworld of your own. She thinks, and I agree, that it's time you started to meet day-to-day living head-on.''

''I don't believe this is Jan's idea,'' Mary stormed. ''She knows how I feel about this house. She would never leave me here alone of her own free will. It's your doing, I know it is!'' If she was being unfair, she was too frantic to care. How would she ever manage to stay on in this house without Jan to stand between her and Barbara?

With Jan here—to run interference, it was true—her dealings with her husband's mistress/ housekeeper had been almost nonexistent, except for that horrible confrontation when she had first arrived; but if Jan left, there was no way she could avoid having to deal with Barbara on a daily basis. She would be forced to observe her and Jamie together, exchanging looks of intimacy, or worse still, trying to conceal those same intimate looks when their bodies or fingers touched in seeming casualness.

It had been difficult enough watching him

cuddle and caress little Jaycie at every opportunity, watching her little face light up whenever he entered a room. He made no effort to hide his love for his second child; and because she, too, had come to love Jaycie, she had resigned herself to seeing them together constantly. But watching him with Barbara was another matter. Mary would never be able to bear the agony of observing him display that same love and tenderness to the child's mother.

And that he would be tender and loving to the mother of his child, she had no doubt. She remembered all too clearly his attitude toward her after Cal had been born. He had treated the birth of their child as a very special gift that she had given him, one for which he could never adequately thank her; and so he had put her on a pedestal, showering her with affection.

At the time she had thought it was just his way of showing his love, but now she knew better. She had given him what he wanted most in the world—a son—and he had shown his gratitude as only a very rich, sensuous man knew how. If she had not discovered his infidelity, she had no doubt that he would still be acting the loving, indulgent husband—the Fitzhughs always paid in full for all favors received. They also never forgave their enemies.

She shivered, realizing that somehow that was what she had now become, while Barbara and Jaycie were the ones basking under his unmatched generosity and sensuous good will.

"I can't stay on in this house if Jan leaves."

The hands in her lap were no longer still but twisted together as she searched for the right words. "I'll pay her salary myself. I have a little money saved." It was a vain promise and they both knew it. She stared wildly into her husband's eyes, trying to hide her fright.

"Jan told me you hated this house," he said as a frown creased his forehead, "but I had no idea it was such an obsession with you. Are you afraid someone will murder you in your bed without her here to protect you?"

She took a deep breath and swallowed convulsively as she clutched at the straw he had thrown her. He mustn't know that it wasn't the house, but its occupants who frightened her. "Yes, yes. That's it. I hate this house and I'm afraid to be alone in it. Sometimes I think it's haunted," she finished with a vague gesture, unable to look him in the eye for fear he would see reflected in hers what really haunted her about the place.

"You're being childish," Jamie said coldly, "but it doesn't matter. You won't be staying here for much longer."

She looked up at him quickly. He was sending her away, then? He unfolded himself from the chair and stretched for a long moment, looking down at her from what seemed like a great height, and gave her a wry smile. "You and I are going to take a trip to Jeff City. The time has come, dear wife, for you to play the part of the loving spouse to the next United States representative from the State of Missouri."

"You want *me* to go with you to Jeff City?" she

repeated stupidly. "But that's impossible. I'm not well. I'm, I'm not—"

He walked over to her chair and drew her unsteadily to her feet. "You're going. We leave next Monday. That gives you a week to have your hair done and do all the foolish things that women do before going on a trip."

"I—I haven't anything to wear." Helplessly she fell back on a woman's oldest excuse.

"Barbara will take you shopping on the Plaza. I've told her you'll need an entire wardrobe for the trip. The few things you've been wearing around here have all seen better days." He did not believe in mincing words. Her meager wardrobe had appalled him, and he was glad of the excuse to force her to replenish it.

Mary's chin tilted dangerously upward. She was no longer frightened; she was furious. "I am *not* going shopping with Barbara!" What she meant was that she was perfectly capable of shopping on her own, but he misinterpreted her meaning.

"Very well. Then Barbara will simply shop for you, and you can take whatever she selects. She has excellent clothes sense, and I'm sure that whatever she selects will be more suitable than what you've been wearing."

She could not believe the gall of the man. Naturally, she had been wearing what little had been salvaged from the fire—old, comfortable clothes—around the house during her convalescence, but that did not mean she did not know how to dress when the occasion warranted it. She might not have a closet full of designer dresses any longer, but careful shopping of the sales at the Jones Store and Macy's had resulted in a wardrobe that had served her well. Of course, she had nothing that could have been worn to the American Royal Ball, but they had been more than adequate for work. And certainly being poor was nothing she had to apologize to him for. Tight-lipped, she rose from the chair.

"And do something about your hair," he continued ruthlessly. "You look like a teenaged hippy with it hanging loose down your back like that."

Once he had loved her long hair. His hands would roam through it at the slightest excuse, and when she tried to tie it back, he would laughingly loosen it and tug the ends of it to pull her to him. Once . . .

"You're right," she agreed. "It needs cutting. I'll make an appointment to have it done tomorrow."

He looked disconcerted, perhaps because she had agreed with him so unexpectedly. "Er, surely that won't be necessary. I had in mind perhaps the way you used to wear it, pulled back and folded in at the nape of your neck," he stumbled along, unfamiliar with the proper female terms for such an arrangement.

"You mean a French twist," she interpreted, shaking her head negatively. "I don't think so. It will be easier just to cut it and forget it."

"No!" he barked, and then carefully controlled his voice. "That is, whatever you prefer, of course, but that—French twist, was it?—creates exactly the right image for the occasion. With a new haircut we don't know what the results would be, do we? And then it would be too late to do anything about it. I think I would prefer the French twist," he concluded after this somewhat wandering explanation, his feeble attempts at diplomacy overcome by his normally arrogant desire to have his own way.

Mary gave a careless shrug. What did it matter? She had agreed to play the dutiful wife and it no longer made any difference to her how she looked. All Jamie was interested in was that she create the "right image" before the selection committee in Jefferson City. With the right clothes and the right hairdo, any woman would do, as long as she remembered to keep smiling and could be depended upon not to make waves. A plastic wind-up doll of a wife was what Jamie wanted of her, and that was what he would get.

"You won't cut it?"

Mary's mind was a million miles away when his abrupt words pulled her back to the present. "No," she agreed with a weary sigh. "Is there anything else?"

"You're still not sulking about Jan?" he probed. The droop of her shoulders disturbed him.

Mary looked up at him blankly for a moment. "Oh, yes, Jan. When did you say she was leaving? I'd like to buy her a present." She hesitated a moment and then, her face burning with embarrassment, she added, "I don't suppose you would loan me ten dollars?"

A look of angry disbelief crossed his face. "You

intend to spend *all* of ten dollars on a present for Jan? Not very generous, are you?''

Mary longed for the floor to open up and swallow her. She would have been better off asking Fitz for the money. "Sh-she knows I don't have any money," she stammered.

"She knows nothing of the sort! Are you trying to make me look like some kind of a fool? You know very well that I opened a checking account in your name at the bank, and I was more than generous.''

She stared up at him, uncomprehending. "I don't have a checking account."

"What kind of a game are you playing now?'' he snapped. "When I pay the household accounts for the month, I also deposit a check in your account. Barbara explained all this to you, I'm sure.''

Barbara again. Mary accepted this bit of information with an eloquent silence that spoke volumes. Furious, Jamie stormed to the doorway and shouted into the empty corridor, "Barbara! Come here at once!''

Within moments the sound of footsteps scurrying toward them could be heard, and then Barbara, flushed, patting her hair into place, entered the room. Her eyes darted nervously from Jamie to Mary and back to Jamie.

"You wanted me, Jamie?'' An uncertain smile flickered over her lips, but the look in her eyes was definitely frightened.

"Mary tells me she knows nothing about the checking account I opened for her. How can that be? You and I discussed this matter in great detail the first day she arrived, didn't we?''

Mary, who was watching the two of them carefully, could have sworn that a look of relief brought color back into Barbara's wan cheeks. "Well, of course we did, Jamie." She smoothed the collar of her dress and looked up at him with a much more confident smile. "I remember telling you at the time how generous I thought you were being," she said in gentle reproach.

"Never mind what you told me," he said grimly. "What did you tell Mary?"

The fingers at her collar stilled. "Why . . . nothing, Jamie. Naturally I assumed that you would talk to Mary about the account yourself. Anything you discussed with me, I assumed was in confidence." From the look that passed between them, Mary was sure that they had discussed many things "in confidence."

Jamie clutched the back of his neck in a gesture of irritation. "I thought I told you to tell her. No matter. In any event, when the statements came back from the bank at the end of the month, surely you must have noticed that no money was being withdrawn. Why didn't you mention it to me?"

Barbara gave Mary a knowing look and then turned her attention back to Jamie. "Well, naturally, I noticed that no money was being used, but I assumed that Mary was saving the money as sort of a nest egg for when she left here, and was relying on . . . that is . . . " She gave Mary another smile, as though they shared a secret. "I assumed you were giving her cash for her day-to-day expenses." She seemed unaware of the fury that was in the look Mary was giving her.

Jamie, however, seemed satisfied with her explanation. "Thank you, Barb. We'll discuss this again later." He started to dismiss her with a wave of his hand but changed his mind and brought that hand to rest gently on her shoulder, staying her from leaving the room.

"By the way, I've told Mary that I want her to have an entirely new wardrobe for our trip. Since she doesn't feel up to shopping yet, I'd appreciate it if you would take care of the matter for her as soon as possible and let me—that is, let *us*—see what you've purchased. I believe I still have charge accounts open at Adler's and Swanson's that you can use.

"Yes, I've used them before." She threw an insolent glance in Mary's direction before returning her gaze to Jamie. She patted his hand in a placating gesture. "You can depend on me."

I'll just bet he can, Mary thought angrily. Then she realized that she and Jamie were alone again, and an uneasy silence fell between them.

At last Jamie spoke. "I'm sorry about the mix-up." He gave her a puzzled look. "You should have said something."

"I'm sorry that the matter even came up now," she confessed miserably. "I don't want your money. I don't even want the ten dollars. I'm sure your gift will be so generous, anything I could give her would seem ridiculous in comparison."

Jamie put one finger under her chin and lifted

her face toward him so that he could see if the expression in her eyes matched the woebegone tone of her voice. Deliberately she made her features a bland mask. There was no way she was going to allow him to see how much it hurt her to learn that Barbara had access to his charge accounts, even though she had suspected as much.

He sensed her withdrawal and it angered him. What did the woman want of him? He had gone out of his way to placate her, and she refused to give an inch. His finger tightened on her chin, holding her gaze, his eyes narrowing as they roamed over her tense, rigid body, drinking in the petal softness of her skin, savoring its perfume that was as familiar to him as the air he breathed ... and as precious.

His hands longed to slip down the fragile column of that exquisite white neck, to find the pulse point that lay dormant there and feel it race away at his touch. At the same time he wanted to strangle her for getting under his skin this way. Did she have any idea how she was tearing him apart? Every time she looked at him, his defenses crumbled just a little bit more. If he weren't careful—

He stopped short. But, of course, he was careful. He didn't give a damn about her. Why should he care what she wanted? He was using her, he reminded himself defiantly, and they had both better remember that before the situation got out of hand.

His eyes darkened in remembered contempt. "Take the money, sweetheart," he said silkily. "I guarantee you'll earn every penny of it before your stay here is through.'' Then, flipping her chin loose of his grip, he turned on his heels and left her alone in the room.

Chapter Eight

Mary sat grimly beside Jamie in the low-slung sports car, which he was driving much too swiftly down the narrow, winding road that spanned the distance between Kansas City and the state Capitol. He had always been a fast driver, but he was positively maniacal now. If she hadn't been too angry at him to even speak, she would have been entreating him to slow down; but she was still simmering over the way he had ridden roughshod over her wishes and practically shanghaied her on this trip.

Mary still could not believe that he had forced her to accept the ridiculous wardrobe that Barbara had selected for her, which she absolutely loathed. Every item of it was totally unbecoming to her in one subtle way or another. She had tried to include some of her own things when she was packing, but Jamie had spotted them and relegated them to the ragbag. Her best dresses to the ragbag by a pompous man who apparently judged good taste by the amount of money spent on a garment! Well, he would have a rude awakening coming to him and sooner than he would like!

Her mutinous thoughts were interrupted when the car swerved wildly to avoid hitting a large mud turtle that was plodding its way across the road, throwing her roughly against the arm that Jamie had flung out to stop her from falling against the windshield. Well, he might have saved her from a nasty bump on the forehead, but her breasts stung from the sharp contact with his stiffly outstretched arm.

"Are you okay?" He threw her a worried glance out of the corner of his eye before returning his concentration to the road ahead.

"Fool!" she snapped, pushing the offending arm away as she struggled to regain her composure. "You could have killed us both." Immediately she regretted breaking her vow of silence and pursed her lips together, determined not to make the same mistake again.

He gave her another quizzical look. "Would you have wanted me to run over the poor thing? That doesn't sound like the tender-hearted Manya I remember." He was baiting her deliberately, but she ignored him.

He knew perfectly well that she did not want to be here, and although he could force her to accompany him, there was no way she was going to engage in idle chitchat with him. He had been ruthless in depriving her of Jan's company and comfort, and callous in forcing her to leave Cal behind when she had wanted to take him with them; but forcing her to wear Barbara's clothes—

and she would never think of them as anything
else—was the last straw.

The memory of him gathering up her own pitifully few things and thrusting them into Barbara's
arms with instructions to "get rid of them," and
the amused condescension in Barbara's eyes as
she had complied, still made her face burn. He
had thought nothing of humiliating his wife in
front of his housekeeper-cum-mistress.

As if that were not bad enough, she had had to
sit primly in the living room and endure the sight
of Barbara parading the unending number of outfits that she had selected for Mary to take with her
on the trip, supposedly for Mary's approval, but
most certainly her attentions the entire time had
been concentrated on Jamie, who sat through the
whole procedure with quiet patience, obviously
enjoying the evidence of his own largesse and
oblivious of Mary's boredom and mounting fury.
"Pompous idiot," she murmured under her
breath, remembering the scene.

"Did you say something?" Jamie asked innocently, taking his eyes off the road to look in her
direction. The look she returned was more eloquent than anything she could have said, and he
quickly turned his attention back to the road, but
not before she saw the beginnings of a smile tug at
the corners of his mouth.

Dismissing the present from her mind, she returned to her own dark thoughts. For all his supposed cleverness, he had allowed Barbara to talk
him into buying two giant suitcases full of the ugli-
est clothes she had ever seen, including the hide-

ous creation she was now wearing. The dresses had all been of the finest fabrics, from the most exclusive designers, and cost a small fortune; and all of them were totally wrong for her willowy figure and fragile features.

She wrinkled her nose as she looked down at the raw silk suit she was now wearing. Anyone looking at it could tell its worth, and the material was exquisite; and yet, its harsh shade of yellow made her honey-blond hair seem brassy; the slit in the tight, straight skirt showed too much thigh; and the deep V-necked jacket exposed too much cleavage. Short puffed sleeves added the final hideous touch. Perhaps Barbara's tiny lush figure could do justice to this outfit and the others like it, but Mary felt like a rock-star groupie. And judging from the startled look in Jamie's eyes when he had first seen her in this suit, she was sure that a similar thought had passed through his mind as well.

Yet, with typical male logic, he had been angry with *her* for the way she looked in the suit, which he had forced her to wear; that, she was sure, was the reason for his unbelievable reckless driving. Her lips curved into a small smile at the thought that at least she had managed to upset him. If he insisted on trying to run her life to the extent of having his mistress pick out her clothes, then he could very well live with the results. It would be interesting to see what his fine political friends would make of her weird wardrobe.

Their imagined reaction helped to erase the memory of the malicious look that Barbara had

furtively bestowed upon her while displaying her
purchases to Jamie with an air of deceptive coop-
eration. Barbara had known exactly how each outfit would look on Mary when she bought them,
and her look had told her as much; but Mary had
been helpless to do anything about it in view of
Jamie's satisfaction with Barbara's assistance. Yes,
she decided, it was all Jamie's fault for being such
a dupe, and now he could just face the ridicule of
his fancy influential friends when they saw how
his wife looked.

"You're doing this deliberately to get back at
me, aren't you?" Jamie rubbed the back of his
neck with long strong fingers. It was a familiar gesture, indicating the tension that was building up
inside him. Once she would have assuaged that
tension by rubbing the back of his shoulders while
he drove; now she hoped he would have a stiff
neck that lasted their entire trip. She looked away
quickly, ignoring his question.

"Damn it, Mary, you look like a tart in that
dress," he blurted out. "The minute we get to the
hotel, you're changing into something else."

She smiled to herself. He had quite a surprise
coming when he saw what the other dresses
looked like on her. This "sunburst creation" had
been the most subdued of the lot. She bit her lip
to keep her smile from spreading, but his alert
storm-cloud eyes had not missed her expression.

With a very explicit curse he pulled the car off
the road onto the dirt shoulder, slammed on the
parking brake, and turned it off. Then he turned
to her and reached out to twist her toward him

with very ungentle hands, his fingers digging through the puffed sleeves to bruise the soft flesh beneath.

"They're all like that, aren't they? You're determined to ruin my chances with the committee."

The unfairness of his remark made her forget she was not speaking to him. "*I* didn't buy those horrid clothes. Your precious Barbara did."

She saw his eyes narrow as they registered the truth of her remark, but he did not apologize. The Fitzhughs did not apologize easily, if at all; she had long ago learned that. "Well, we'll just have to turn back as far as Sedalia and pick up some clothes in one of the shops there. We are not arriving in Jeff City with you looking like that," he snapped. "And this time, you'll try on each item before I approve the purchase."

"Sedalia," she jibed, "that's just a small farming community. Surely you don't expect them to have anything comparable to the designer fashions you obtained on the Plaza."

"If you're referring to what you're now wearing," he sneered, "I'm sure anything they have will be an improvement." Without a further word he restarted the car, turning it around in the direction they had just come, back toward Sedalia, which was at least twenty miles away.

As they drove down the wide main street that cut through the center of Sedalia, Jamie's alert eyes picked out a small sign advertising a woman's boutique in the middle of a busy shopping area. Parking the car with a minimum of motion in front of the shop, he hustled a protesting Mary into it.

When the saleslady looked up to see a glowering stranger, half dragging a young lady into her shop, she did not know what to expect. He looked fierce enough to be a burglar, but the expensive cut of his clothes quickly disabused her of that apprehensive thought. The young woman with him was wearing an atrocious outfit, for all that it must have cost more than an entire rack of the dresses she carried in the shop. She was not at all surprised when the man told her that he wanted something entirely different for his wife to wear and then proceeded to explain exactly what he had in mind. She thanked her lucky stars that she had just returned from a buying trip to Chicago, or she would have been no help to him at all.

She tried not to stare at the wife, who was obviously not in the least interested in clothes, but she could not help wondering about her. Her handsome husband obviously adored her—or why else would he be spending a fortune on her clothes?—but she seemed very unhappy about something. Well, the saleswoman clucked to herself, it took all kinds, but if that hunk of man were hers...

She brought herself up sharply and concentrated on searching through her back room for some of the newest items to bring out for his inspection. It was a pleasure to watch a man so interested in everything his wife wore. He examined the colors and the fabrics with a careful eye, and even then he insisted that his wife model each item for his loving approval before he made the final selections.

The saleswoman prided herself on knowing her business, and each item that she persuaded Mary to try on was more flattering than the one before, and it was not long before the young couple, despite the wife's protests, had bought most of the shop's new spring collection.

When they emerged from the shop an hour later, Jamie's arms were laden with packages and Mary was wearing a beige linen dress, trimmed with tiny russet buttons down the front and a narrow russet belt at the waist, its simple lines accented by a designer scarf of plaid silk loosely knotted over the small rolled collar. They left behind them a bewildered saleswoman who was torn between the pleasure over the largest sale she had ever made and the realization that she would have to make another buying trip to restock her boutique.

Back in the car, driving once more toward Jefferson City, Mary could not resist asking, "What will you do with all those other dresses?"

"Barbara bought them, and she can damn well get rid of them," he replied angrily. "She can burn them, or return them, or wear them, for all I care."

"I'm sure that's exactly what she had in mind," Mary answered sweetly.

He threw her an indignant look. "Now, don't blame Barb for this. She couldn't have known how those dresses would look on you any more than I could. She went out of her way to be helpful and she spared no expense on your behalf," he defended.

She gave a heavy sigh. Of course his Barbara could do no wrong.

Unwisely, Jamie pressed the issue. "You should have said the clothes were all wrong for you."

If looks could kill, he would have had a heart attack. Mary turned her back to him and stared determinedly out the window. He was impossible.

With a look of disgust in the direction of her stiff shoulders, Jamie turned his attention back to the road. So, she was back on the silent kick, was she? There was no pleasing her. Women were supposed to love pretty clothes, weren't they? And hadn't he just bought her two complete wardrobes in as many days? Instead of being pleased, she was sulking again.

Jamie threw her another sideways glance. Mary's face was carefully turned away from him, but the sunlight playing in the twist of her honey-colored hair held his attention for a long moment. Did it still feel like cornsilk? he wondered. Did it still smell faintly of lily of the valley? Damn.

He brought his eyes quickly back to the road in front of him and his knuckles whitened around the rim of the steering wheel. What did a man have to do to get the smell and the feel of her out of his mind? Every moment he was with her it became harder to remember that she had betrayed him. He found himself staring at her like a gawky schoolboy, wanting her to smile at him, to talk to him, the way she used to. He still remembered the way it was; there was never enough time in a day to share all the things they saved up for each other. They would find themselves talking as they made love, not caring about the actual words, but basking in the soft exchange that bound them together.

In a burst of defiance his foot pressed the gas pedal to the floor, commanding the car to leap forward over the lonely road. He'd be damned if he'd let her shut him out now.

A gasp of horror escaped Mary's white lips as she watched the speedometer climb past one hundred. They would both be killed if he didn't let up.

"Please, Jamie," she pleaded, all thoughts of ignoring him wiped from her mind.

To her relief his foot eased up on the gas pedal as he carefully brought himself and the car under control. She gave him an accusing look, but did not dare voice her anger. He seemed immensely pleased with himself for having pierced her icy reserve.

"What shall we talk about?" he blackmailed in his most agreeable voice.

She knew better than to protest now, and reluctantly, she allowed him to lead her into a conversation about their forthcoming meeting with the political leaders waiting for them in Jeff City. Surprisingly she found herself listening with rapt interest as he described the purpose of their meeting, the people they would be seeing, what they expected of him and of her, and what he hoped to achieve with their support.

That he would make a very good representative for Jackson County, she had no doubt. Jamie was very knowledgeable about the problems of the area soy bean farmers and the small business communities such as Belton and Grandview, and equally well informed on the big city problems facing Kansas City itself. When she had lived with him, he had been an ambitious young lawyer; somewhere along the way he had become a very concerned citizen.

Mary realized, almost against her will, that anyone listening to him present his ideas would be as mesmerized as she was by the throaty timbre of his voice, which was both magnetic and sincere. Even hating him as she did, she found herself falling under the spell of his dreams for the area and would no doubt vote for him if he secured the party nomination. What chance did other, more impartial observers have of resisting his appeal?

As they drove up in front of the rounded tower that was the local Holiday Inn, she knew a momentary pang of regret that the trip was ending. What was the matter with her? How could she have forgotten, even for a moment, that this was the man who had betrayed her? No doubt, if elected to office, he would betray the voters as well, despite his silver tongue. She set her lips in a cold, determined line, which erased the soft, relaxed look her face had assumed, and their temporary truce was over.

In fact, it burst into all-out warfare when they reached their suite of rooms. Following dutifully behind the bellcap, it was soon apparent that other than a very large sitting room and a luxurious bath, there was only one bedroom. She turned in a fury to face Jamie, who was calmly dismissing the bellcap with a tip large enough to draw a salute before he withdrew.

Hands on hips, eyes blazing, Mary strode to within inches of the infuriating man who towered over her, smiling blandly. "There is only *one* bedroom," she stormed.

"It has two very comfortable double beds," he pointed out reasonably, totally unmoved by her outrage. "After all, we are supposed to be a happily reconciled couple."

"Then this arrangement is no surprise to you," she sputtered. "You knew all along—"

"Do you want the bed nearest the bathroom?" He ignored her objections with an indulgent smile. "As I remember, you often get up in the middle of the night."

"That was only when I was pregnant," she snapped with an indignant stamp of her foot, somewhat nonplussed that he should have remembered such an intimate detail. She fought down a blush and brought the conversation back to the cause of her present anger. "And I do not intend to share any part of this bedroom with you. I'll call down to the desk and arrange for another room."

He reached down to grasp her shoulders with rough, punishing hands. "You will do nothing of the sort. The happily married Fitzhughs will share the same room now and whenever we happen to be away from home overnight. Do you understand?" The ice in his voice told her the matter was not open for further discussion. "The time has come, my dearest wife, for you to pay your dues."

Yes, she thought wearily, everything he had done for her since the accident—the medical bills he had taken care of, arranging for Jan's services, giving her a roof over her head in which to recuperate, allowing her to get to know her son again—all those things had been in deliberate, calculated preparation for this moment when he would need a loving wife at his side to impress the central committee. He had made it plain from the very first what her role was to be and he was not now about to back down from his demands.

"V-very well," she conceded, "but just remember that this is all a business arrangement. If you so much as touch me..." she threatened.

She should have known better; Jamie had never responded well to threats. A furious scowl crossed his set features, erasing the civilized veneer.

"I am touching you this very minute," he challenged, his thumbs tracing tantalizing circles into the soft flesh of her shoulders. "What are you going to do about it?"

Mary tried to escape the insidious seduction of his touch, but it was soon apparent that he was not going to allow her to move. Defiantly she threw her head back in a scornful gesture calculated to wither him where he stood. Another mistake. When her eyes locked with his, it was she who was lost. The iceberg-gray depths that blazed back at her with a sudden naked desire shocked her into revealing an answering blaze in her own eyes. Quickly she lowered her lids, turning away before he could see too much. But it was too late.

He *had* seen and quickly moved to take advantage. One hand left her shoulder to slide down her back to the curve of her hips, forcing her body to mold into his, while the fingers of the other hand splayed themselves against a throbbing breast.

"I intend to keep touching you," Jamie uttered hoarsely, the long months of his self-imposed control shattered beyond all repair, "until you beg me not to stop." His mouth descended ruthlessly, irreversibly, to claim hers. The fingers on her shoulders slipped down to the front of her dress and found her breasts, the warmth of his hands penetrating the layers of material to blaze on her flesh.

Her breath caught in her throat and her hands fluttered ineffectively at his chest, attempting to push him away. Then the tangy masculine odor of his body invaded her senses, and without volition her arms made their own treasonous way up and around his neck and locked there, even as her lips moved in protest. "Please, Jamie."

He gave a husky laugh of triumph. "See, you're begging already." He gave her a gentle shove toward the nearest bed, and the two of them tumbled down on to it, still locked in each other's arms.

"This is the bed we'll *both* share for the entire trip," he informed her with lazy assurance as he loosened the scarf from around her neck and investigated the row of tiny buttons that started there.

"No," she tried again to protest. "I d-don't w-want..."

"Liar," he drawled into her ear, his breath hot and disturbing against her skin. "You've 'wanted' ever since the moment I held you under the shower. I'm the one that's been playing hard to get. But you've got me now. I'm not as immune to you as I thought."

"Nooo," she moaned, stung by his arrogant assumption that she was his for the taking, yet her arms around his neck held on with a will of their own. Her body trembled, but did not resist, as he pushed her unbuttoned dress down over her hips and flung it on the floor. For a moment she lay there, clad only in a lacy bra and bikini underpants as his eyes glittered down on her.

"This is how I remember you best," he breathed heavily, "your body bared to me—waiting for me to bring it to life. I've had enough of that cold, aloof ghost you've turned into." He disposed of the remaining wisps of lace as he talked, leaving her naked to his devouring eyes. With an oath he pressed her quivering body deeply against his own fully clad, taut form, their heartbeats mingling until the sound magnified in her ears, like the roar of a waterfall that she was drowning in.

His hands roamed all over her—touching, lingering, rediscovering—and his mouth destroyed hers with its moist, possessive probing. And, heaven help her, she returned his kisses hungrily. Years of deprivation and abstinence took their toll and demanded relief. She clung to him, moaning under his mouth, writhing under his hands. Whatever happened afterward, however much she hated herself later, she had to know his body just once more. In a frenzy of surrender she arched up to meet the calculated demands of his passion.

Her mouth reached up for his and she kissed his stiff lips again and again and again. With trembling fingers she undid the buttons of his shirt and placed her lips against the nipples of his chest, where they lay hidden in his thick mat of curly hair, kissing one and then the other in lingering, desperate caresses. Her fingers reached down and undid the buckle of his belt and slid down the zipper of his slacks.

The touch of her fingers slipping below his waist broke the iron control he had imposed on himself, and he pushed her hands away in a frenzy to remove his clothes and claim her body. Painfully his hands twisted in her hair, undoing its neat chignon and letting the hair fall freely around them. He forced her face up to accept his rough, demanding kisses as he rammed his body into hers.

It was angry, hateful loving—primitive in its fury and irresistible in its urgency—and neither of them would have had it any other way. Their bodies were locked together in triumphant defiance of their common sense and they reveled in a possession of each other that would not have been possible if they had been thinking rationally. He carried her with him down familiar paths of ecstasy that she had almost forgotten; and when she cried out at the wonder of it, he licked her tears away with a possessive tongue that wanted to taste every part of her.

Neither of them spoke. To do so would have meant a return to sanity and would have driven them apart, and they could not bear for anything to part them just yet.

Finally they fell asleep locked in each other's arms. They slept a long time as though they were afraid to wake up and face the consequences of their unbelievable behavior.

Chapter Nine

Mary awoke first. She knew instantly where she was, what she had done. Her face burned with shame, but her arms remained locked around Jamie's neck while her face lay buried in the spiky hair of his chest. She did not dare move for fear of waking him and facing the enormity of what had happened between them. How could she have allowed herself to be swept along in such a maelstrom of unreasoning passion?

"You're awake," a sleepy voice observed tenderly from somewhere above her head.

"How—how did you know?"

"Your eyelashes are tickling my chest." She could feel the smile in his words. Embarrassed, she tried to move away.

"Not yet." His arms tightened around her possessively, and she felt his body harden as he drew her closer.

"We must have been crazy." The words came out in a croak past her dry lips.

"If so, then I still am. I've been lying here waiting for you to wake up. I want to make love with you again." His voice was as unsteady as her own as his hands slid down to her waist and maneuvered her body until she was lying on top of him.

"What are you doing?" she protested as his hands pressed her hips into his.

He gave her a lazy smile and then lifted his head so that his tongue traced slow patterns around her rapidly hardening nipples. She raised herself on stiffened elbows, trying to evade him, but succeeded only in giving him easier access to her firm breasts. Her hair fell around them like a curtain, shutting out the rest of the room, the rest of the world.

"We can't," she protested uncertainly.

One of his hands left her hips and came to rest in the nape of her neck, forcing her very gently toward him again. "We *are*," he corrected with a throaty drawl.

His gentleness confused her. If he were still the wild man who had possessed her so savagely only a short time before, she would have been able to cope with that, but instead he was disarming her with a softness she had not seen in him for a long time.

"We just can't make love again," she tried helplessly to explain. "It should never have happened in the first place; but to do it again, that would be monstrous!"

"Mmmm," he agreed, stroking her hair. His mouth did not release its rosy prize.

"No. Don't do that!" Mary cried out in alarm as she realized that his other hand was trailing sensuously along the inner softness of her thighs, stirring responses she had thought satiated by their early lovemaking. Spasms of delight ran down the entire length of her body, forcing her to curl and uncurl her toes in a futile effort to retain her self-control.

At the same time she was not unaware that in this mood, Jamie was leaving the decision up to her. His kisses were gently persistent, his hands subtly insistent; and though his body surged against hers, she knew he was in better control of his emotions than she was and would bring the proceedings to an abrupt halt if she so demanded.

They were in the midst of a choreographed dance that they had done together many times before, and each knew the other's steps by heart. His hands stroked over the length of her body, slipping in and around the inner warmth of her thighs, making her aware that he wanted her, while the warm breath of his mouth, hovering over her breast, seemed to be mutely asking if she wanted him. Her little moans of either protest or passion did not adequately answer his query.

She knew she had only to put her hands on his shoulder and lever herself away and the dance would be ended. She meant to do exactly that and started to push away from him, but the sweetness of his touch on her thighs, the thrusting surge of her nipples toward the hot promise of his mouth, would not be denied. In a fever of emotion she found herself falling forward across his body and his arms coming up to enfold her in a giant bear hug.

"Yes?" he inquired triumphantly.

"Yesss," she breathed into his ear and then hid her burning face from those glittering eyes.

The sun was lower in the sky now, and they were both awake, still locked in each other's arms, watching the patterns it made on the wall.

"It's getting late." Jamie broke the silence with reluctance. "We have that damn dinner date to keep."

She did not answer, but involuntarily her body stiffened. His words had brought the outside world back into their stolen moment out of time and space. "I'll get dressed, then." Her voice was dull, the magic gone.

"No." Sensing her mood, he changed his mind and pulled her back to him. "Perhaps we should talk first." He flicked an impatient glance at the slim gold watch on his wrist, as though it were deliberately trying to annoy him. "It's only five," he said firmly, ignoring its demand for action. "We can get a lot of things settled between us before we meet the others at eight."

"What is there to settle?" she said tonelessly, her body still rigid against his. "Nothing has changed. We both just suffered a temporary lapse of memory. It didn't mean anything."

"Didn't it?" he probed. "Then I must have been imagining the wild excitement, the pleasure, the unbelievable sensations, we just shared. Are you trying to tell me it wasn't the same for you? If so, you're wasting your breath. I *know* what happened to you. Why, you haven't even come down yet; your skin is still moist with perspiration and hot to my touch and you've got a raspberry rash on your chest.''

She trembled under the truth of his analysis. ''Oh, no,'' she groaned. ''I ought to hate you.''

''I know,'' he soothed, patting her head as though she were his child. ''I really do. I ought to hate you, too; but I can't.'' His arms folded her against him and he rocked her to him comfortingly until she relaxed and curled her body into his. How could she deny that this was where she wanted to be, had to be, where she belonged?

''That's right. Relax. Everything is going to be all right for us, I promise.'' She did not reply, but he did not seem to mind. He continued to hold her possessively with an absence of desire, his mind a million miles away, trying to find the solution he had promised her.

He was silent so long, she thought he must have fallen asleep again, when he gave her a quick, triumphant squeeze and sat up in the bed, pulling her up with him and cradling her in his lap.

''You and I,'' he declared with the confidence of one who had just deciphered the Rosetta stone, ''have been going about this entirely the wrong way! We've been trying to live within the confines of a very unstable and, let's admit it, unsatisfactory marriage, when what we need to do is to have an affair!''

She turned the full force of her luminous aquamarine gaze on him. ''I don't even think that's funny.''

The misery in her eyes made him hasten to kiss her quickly, almost chastely, on the forehead. "No, honey. Don't look at me like that. I meant with each other, of course."

She was thoroughly confused now. "We *are* still married, aren't we?"

His mouth came searching for hers and found it in a soothing kiss. "Of course we are. That's our trouble. We hate being married to each other. Marriage implies commitment and promises to be kept—all the things we've failed at in the past."

The things you've *failed at*, she wanted to protest, but his fingers on her lips stilled her words.

"It's true and you know it. We hurt each other and blamed each other for breaking our marriage vows so often in the past that there wasn't room left for anything but hatred between us. That's why we need to forget the past, forget any sense of obligation or duty toward each other, and simply enjoy the uncomplicated relationship of an affair." When she continued to stare at him uncomprehendingly, he continued with a patient explanation. "In an affair two people simply enjoy sex together without making any other demands on each other."

"And have you had many such affairs?" she demanded coolly, her body tensing in his arms.

"Ha!" he laughed, his fingers chastising her rump with a playful slap. "Now, that's a very wifely question. And do you see its effect? Just asking it makes your body stiff and hostile. One doesn't ask questions about the past in an affair.

An affair is a 'for now' thing between two people, with no explanations demanded or given on either side. When you have to ask 'Is there someone else?' the affair is automatically over. Don't you see how simple it is?''

"What you're trying to say is that in one of these affairs, one doesn't have to be faithful," she said scornfully. "How convenient for you."

A shadow crossed his face and for a moment she thought she had struck a nerve and angered him. She could sense the tight control in his voice as he continued.

"Well, for some people fidelity is certainly not a requirement," he admitted, "but in our case, I think it would be best if we did try to be faithful to each other. I don't have anyone else on the string right now, do you?" There was a tightness around his mouth as he waited for her answer.

"No," she said abruptly.

So, he had no one on the string right now. Was Barbara so much a part of his life, then, that he expected Mary to make an exception for that particular relationship, or was he trying to tell her that Barbara was no longer a part of his life at all? She did not have the courage to ask. He was too close, his body too comfortable as he curled her into its rugged planes, for her to say the words that would drive them apart.

Still, she could not dismiss Barbara completely from her thoughts. "It would never work."

"It's working now," he argued. "We're both exactly where we want to be at this moment. The

beauty of it is that we don't have to look beyond
the moment. When it's over, it's over. But we'll
have enjoyed each other in the interim.''

"The whole idea is ridiculous.'' She faltered.
"What you're asking is impossible. Before long
we'd be at each other's throats again.''

"Don't you see what you're doing?'' he pointed out. "You're trying to see into the future. I'm
trying to tell you that it's now that counts. If we
both think of it that way, when it finally does end,
we can simply accept that fact without tears, or
recrimination, or guilt on either side. I'm not asking anything of you, but that you be faithful to me
now; and I promise you the same. When either of
us finds it impossible to keep that promise, the
affair will be over, but not before then.''

"It's impossible to argue with a trial lawyer,''
she groaned, "no matter how foolish his argument. I never even made the high school debating
team.''

He laughed exultantly. "I can feel you smiling.
You like the idea, don't you?''

"I can't believe we're having this conversation.'' He was right, she was smiling; perhaps she
was on the verge of hysteria.

"Can't you?'' he replied. "All I know is that I
have never had better sex in my life than we have
just shared, and I am not about to give it up.''

Of course. That's all this was about to him—
sex. There was no question of love between them
any longer. He had grown past that stage in their
relationship and he was asking her to do the same.
Her heart ached as his lips brushed over her eye-

brows and down to the velvet lids she had closed against him. She wanted to pull away, but both of them knew that she would not.

"God, you're sweet," he moaned against her mouth.

Still she protested. "I'm your wife. I don't understand what would be different if I called myself your mistress." It was a wonder she could think at all with his kisses all over her face.

He gave a short laugh. "Haven't you been listening to anything I've said? My wife and I just don't get along"—his voice was rueful—"and there doesn't seem to be a thing that either of us can do about it. I've long ago resigned myself to that, and I guess she has, too." Mary started to protest, but his fingers on her mouth silenced her.

"Sorry, but that's the way it is and we both know it. Anyway, I've found that the best way to forget an unhappy marriage is with a lighthearted affair with no 'forever after' promises." His steel-gray eyes looked deep into her soul. "And I very much want to have such an affair with you."

So that was how he excused his unfaithfulness over the years—by blaming her for their unhappy marriage. Angrily Mary tried to twist away from him, but he would not let her loose.

"Oh, no, love. There's no room for wifely indignation in this bed," he said sardonically, reading her mind. "You and I are just two lovers basking in the afterglow of a fantastic experience, and we're making plans to do it again and again and again." His hand cupped her breast and allowed the thumb on its rosy nipple to bring it to instant arousal. "Will you be my lover, Manya? For as long as this feeling flares between us?" he asked in a husky, almost pleading whisper.

Mary wanted to rant and rail at him, scratch and bite and even kill him for his assumptions, but her body had already accepted his offer and she found herself slipping one silken leg between his, her toes caressing the foot that was entangled with hers. "Oh, Jamie." She sighed. "This will never work, but for as long as it does, I'll be yours."

"Mine alone?" he insisted savagely.

"Yours alone," she promised against his mouth, but even as she lost herself in the bliss of his kiss, she realized with a pang that he had made no such promise to her.

It didn't matter. What was between them was too strong to be denied or qualified. She did not know how long this euphoria would last, but for now the only thing that mattered was the physical satisfaction they needed from each other. Somewhere along the way they had lost love and trust and respect, yet still they continued to be irresistibly drawn together, and she could fight it no longer.

"I need you so," he whispered harshly, almost accusingly, into her ear.

"I need you, too," she admitted, blinking back tears because that was all they had left between them.

Abruptly his mood changed and he gave her a quick slap on her bare bottom and broke their embrace. "We have got to meet with the committee in an hour, and we barely have time to shower and change. "This"—he dropped a quick kiss on her breast—"will just have to wait a few hours. We've got all the time in the world ahead of us now," he told her, his voice suddenly light-hearted.

"You're right," she agreed, striving for the same casualness he had achieved. "Do you want to shower first, or shall I?"

"What a short memory you have," he drawled as he drew her up from the bed and pulled her with him toward the shower stall.

When they walked into the dining room an hour later, they made a striking couple. Jamie was wearing a dark blue business suit, complete with vest and a narrow silk tie, its conservative pattern accentuating the pristine whiteness of his shirt. Clinging to his arm was a radiant Mary, wearing one of the outfits he had selected for her earlier that day—a plum velvet evening skirt, topped with a silk mauve blouse with capped sleeves and a boat neckline. Her hands were carefully encased in an exquisite pair of mauve lace gloves that she had insisted on purchasing when he bought the skirt. Despite Jamie's warm reassurances, she was very sensitive about her misshapen hands and could not bring herself to bare her scars to strangers.

Around her neck she wore a thick gold chain. Jamie had been wearing it earlier and he had insisted on transferring it to her while they were both in the shower. The chain, he explained, had been a gift from his mother several years ago, but now he wanted her to have it as a token of their new status.

"Lovers should exchange tokens," he informed her solemnly.

"But I haven't anything to give you" had been her dismayed rejoinder as the chain changed owners under the heavy mist of the shower.

His gray eyes had twinkled with mischief as they followed the short chain to its resting place on the high swell of her gleaming wet breasts. "Don't worry, you'll think of something before the evening is through," he assured her.

She had flushed and stood very still as his long fingers adjusted the chain one more time, lingering there. "As long as you wear this, I'll know the affair is still on." His voice choked and he had to clear his throat before continuing. "And right now, I hope you wear it forever."

The chain had sizzled on her wet skin like a tongue of flame, scorching her with its message. It was almost as though it were a form of wedding ring; and yet, that was absurd. He was the one who had insisted on no promises and no long-term commitments. What did he mean, then, by confusing her with such words as *forever*? There could be no forever for them. Just a passion-filled present.

"I think *forever* is a commitment word," she had managed to say with surprising lightness, "don't you?"

The corners of his mouth had tightened ominously for a moment, but then he gave a harsh laugh. "You're learning fast, Manya. Well, instead, let's just hope our affair will last for as long as it takes the chain to tarnish.''

That's strange, she had thought to herself, *doesn't he know that if the chain is gold, it will never tarnish?* However, aloud she had said nothing. Jamie had already reached past her for a towel and it was obvious he had dismissed the subject from his mind.

Now, as they walked into the dining room, she felt a fresh attack of nerves. She looked up at him, and he read the unspoken question in their depths. With a grin he drew her arm more firmly through his and patted it with assurance. "They'll love you," he promised.

Her gloved fingers dug into his hand and she squeezed hard, drawing strength from him. "Sure they will." She laughed shakily and allowed him to lead her to the head table.

At once it was obvious to Mary that the main topic at this dinner was to be the suitability of their prospective candidate's wife for the political arena; and to that end, they were here to judge for themselves exactly what their marital status really was and how it would affect the campaign. The men greeted her politely and then turned to Jamie to discuss people and places she was unaware of. The real business of the evening they left to their wives, who were frankly curious and did not bother to disguise it.

"You don't wear a wedding ring, my dear?" Mrs. Ohlsen, who was obviously their spokeswoman, led the inquisition.

Mary had not been expecting that question

and for one horrible moment she thought her scarred and warped fingers must be visible. She looked down at her hands in dismay, but the sight of the lace gloves, still firmly in place, reassured her. Mrs. Ohlsen was simply on a fishing expedition. Yet she had a point. How could she and Jamie have forgotten a detail as important as a wedding ring? One gloved hand curved instinctively around the gold chain at her neck for support.

Before she could answer, she felt Jamie's huge hand covering hers, lifting her wrist to his lips. "Her doctor's the villain, I'm afraid. Mary is forbidden to wear jewelry of any kind on her hands until the scar tissue has healed completely; and even then, perhaps not until after the plastic surgery restores her fingers to their former smoothness. Her wedding ring wouldn't fit her now, even if it weren't dangerous." He smiled reassuringly into Mary's eyes, and she knew he was telling her not to worry, that no matter how distracted he might appear, he wouldn't desert her. She gave him a grateful look. *Ask away, ladies,* she thought with a suppressed giggle. *The two of us can handle the lot of you.*

Mrs. Ohlsen did just that. "Oh, yes, that dreadful accident. You could have been killed. But then, if there had not been a fire, your husband never would have found you, would he?" Her shrewd brown eyes searched Mary's for a reaction.

"Yes," Mary agreed, "that fire certainly changed my life." She remembered that Jamie had released a story that she had had amnesia, and added, "Seeing Jamie again brought the past all back to me. We're both very happy now," she finished truthfully.

"What about the life you made for yourself when you had no memory of him?" Mrs. Ohlsen persisted. "A pretty thing like you must have had a slew of new boyfriends."

Mary gave a self-deprecating laugh. "I'm afraid not. I did have a job as a bookkeeper in a small firm, and my former employer was certainly very understanding about my lack of references, but I guess I was so confused about my lack of memory that I never was relaxed enough to make new friends. I was rather lonely, actually," she remembered wistfully.

"The apartment you lived in"—Mrs. Ohlsen was like a dog with a bone—"I understand it was quite expensively furnished."

She certainly knew her facts. Mary knew a moment of panic. "They weren't my things," she hastened to say. "I was subletting from..." She hesitated for just a fraction of a second. She could not reveal that she was living with her brother without blowing Jamie's amnesia story full of holes. "... from an engineer who is stationed overseas. Actually, the rent was quite reasonable, since I was supposed to be a sort of caretaker for his valuable collections."

"And what does this engineer think now that all his possessions have been destroyed?"

The inflection on the word *engineer* was almost insulting. What was the woman after? Was there no stopping her pointless questions? Mary threw a frantic look in Jamie's direction, but from the grim set of his features she knew he was not about to help her this time. Not only did he refuse to intervene, but he seemed to be waiting as impatiently as Mrs. Ohlsen for her answer.

"I...I haven't been able to get in touch with him." She chewed her lower lip. "He travels so much, I guess my letters just haven't caught up to him. He was very heavily insured, of course, if that's any consolation to an avid collector. Thank goodness for insurance companies, don't you agree?" she babbled on.

To her intense relief one of the other women took up the conversational gambit from there and proceeded to tell them about the small fire she had had in her kitchen for which the insurance company had paid her enough to remodel the entire kitchen; and much to Mrs. Ohlsen's annoyance, the subject of Mary's involvement with the unknown engineer was forgotten for the moment.

Mary turned an entreating glance in Jamie's direction. Surely he was not going to leave her at their mercy the entire evening. His returning glance was cold, but under the warmth of her silent plea he softened and rose to stand beside her. In the next room the orchestra was playing dance music, and he used that as his excuse.

"If you'll pardon me, gentlemen, I think my wife is asking me to dance; and since this is a sort of second honeymoon for us, I think perhaps I had better oblige."

They laughed appreciatively at his dilemma, and in fact followed his lead and escorted their own wives onto the dance floor. Mary, however, looked questioningly up at her husband as he stood waiting patiently for her to rise.

Did he really expect her to dance? For all practical purposes her leg had healed, but it still ached on occasion and stiffened up on her. She considered herself lucky to have mastered basic walking again; but she definitely was not ready to graduate to ballroom dancing. She gave an almost imperceptible negative shake of her head to indicate that he should sit down beside her, but he chose to ignore it.

"Come on, Manya," he coaxed under a coating of steel, "or this romantic tune will give way to a disco beat, and then you really will have a tough time." But she would still dance was his unspoken message. It was the same tone of voice that he had used to coerce her into taking her meals with him, and she knew the futility of trying to argue with him. With an apprehensive sigh she rose awkwardly, automatically favoring her weaker leg.

"You'll be just fine," Jamie reassured her as his arms wrapped themselves supportively around her waist, holding her to him. They swayed together, barely moving, until her arms crept tightly around his neck and she relaxed sufficiently against the comforting bulwark of his body to follow his lead, and then they blended confidently in among the other dancers.

"Those two kids are very much in love," Milt Ohlsen observed to his wife as they watched the younger couple, wrapped in each other's arms, dance away.

"Are they?" His wife gave him an indulgent smile. "You always were a romantic. But I wonder. Four years is a long time to have a loss of memory. Surely both of them have had the companionship of the opposite sex during that time. We've both seen Jamie out with various women over the past few years. No one serious, I grant you, but what do we know about his wife's activities? You don't want to get stuck with a candidate who might be part of a scandal in November, do you, Milt? If he's nominated, the reporters will be very thorough in their search for dirt."

"Nonsense, Sophie," her husband disclaimed as he continued to watch the Fitzhughs dancing together. Even the woman's slight awkwardness was charming to watch, since it elicited such a protective tenderness in her husband. He felt an uncomfortable twinge of envy. They had everything—each other, beauty, money, and a promising political future. They were a golden couple. "You worry too much. If there were even a hint of scandal attached to those two, the reporters would have filtered it out by now. It's been almost three months since they found each other again. Why, together they have a charisma that will have the voters eating right out of their hands. I think we've got us a winner this time."

"Well, don't say I didn't warn you." She patted his cheek lovingly as she recognized the innocent envy in his eyes. "At least hold off endorsing him just a little longer while you have them investigated yourself. Don't wait for the reporters to do your job for you. If I'm wrong, your endorsement at the end of the month will still be soon enough to be appreciated.

Her husband gave a deep sigh. He knew better than to go against his wife's hunches, but this time he was certain she was wrong. "We'll see," he compromised as his gaze wandered back to the couple in question, where Jamie's sandy head was bent low to rest against his wife's straight blond hair. Such a golden couple.

"What are you thinking about?" Jamie whispered into her ear, his tongue flicking out to lick its lower lobe. "We can leave soon."

"Mrs. Ohlsen doesn't like me," she admitted warily, ignoring his sensual signals. "She doesn't like me and she's suspicious of me."

"Does she have any reason to be?" There was a slight edginess to his voice, which he quickly brought under control when he felt her body stiffen in his arms. He gave a disarming laugh instead. "I don't blame her. Her husband is attracted to you. In fact, every man here has noticed your beauty; therefore, their wives would like to scratch your eyes out. However, we will both reassure them that they have nothing to worry about because very, very soon you will be leaving with me."

"But if they don't like me, it will hurt your career," she worried.

"They'll like you well enough if you ignore their husbands and just sit there looking adoringly at me while I dazzle them with my brilliance."

She laughed in spite of herself. "You're crazy

tonight, do you know that? And I can hardly wait."

He looked down at her for a further explanation of that cryptic statement, and she obliged him by pulling his ear down to her mouth and whispering something that delighted him.

Chapter Ten

"He didn't endorse you!" She echoed his announcement with a groan of despair. "It's all my fault, I know it is."

Jamie did not appear to be at all disconcerted by this turn of events. "He will," he assured her. "I have his promise that he'll come out in my behalf by the end of the month."

"But you expected his endorsement this week," she wailed.

He put a hand to her forehead and brushed an errant lock of silken hair back with his fingertips. "I'm not worried. Milt convinced me that by endorsing me too soon, we might lose our momentum in the campaign's home stretch, and I trust his judgment. Now, don't you think you should pay me the same courtesy—and trust mine?"

"I couldn't bear it if for some reason I caused you to lose their support." Her lower lip quivered. "I did everything I could to make them like me. The lunches, the shopping trips, the bridge games."

"They *loved* you," he assured her emphatically, "and so do—" He stopped short. "So do their wives," he finished lamely. "Now, forget the election for a while and give me a kiss before the bellhop gets here for our bags. The week here is over and it's time we started home."

Home. She lifted her lips dutifully to his, trying not to let him see how the word disturbed her. Home to her was this room, wrapped in his arms with the rest of the world shut out, not the Fitz-hugh mansion, where Barbara and Jaycie waited to remind her of the past she was trying so desperately to forget. She could not control the shadow of doubt that flickered across her face.

"What's wrong?" He had become sensitive to the slightest change in her mood. "I know you hate leaving here; I do, too. But it won't change anything. We'll still be together."

They were so close and yet so far apart. Anything he asked of her she gave willingly, except her innermost thoughts. She sensed that he did the same with her. Only when they made love did they drop their guard, otherwise they were wary of each other and of the chasm that stretched between them that they could not bridge with words. They skirted around issues rather than discuss them, so as not to jeopardize their fragile cease-fire.

"I was thinking of Cal," she lied, "and feeling guilty because I really haven't thought of him at all this week, except for our phone calls to him."

Her attempt to channel the conversation into a safer topic worked, and he gave an indulgent chuckle. "When he's old enough to have a girl of his own, he'll no doubt return the favor by ignoring us."

Except, of course, that there probably would not be any "us" that far in the future, she thought bleakly.

Despite her misgivings, some things simply had to be discussed. "Seriously, Jamie, what are we going to do when we get...back?" She could not bring herself to call Fitz's house home. "About...about us, I mean." She was very embarrassed.

He seemed to have the situation firmly resolved in his own mind. "We're going to move your things into my room, and you're going to tell Cal to start calling you mother, because Manya is my name for you," he said with more than a hint of impatience.

Her worst fears were realized. "We can't," she stumbled. "It wouldn't be fair to get Cal's hopes up about our remaining together when we don't know how long—" Her voice faltered momentarily, but gathering courage, she tried to continue in a lighter vein. "Surely he didn't call your other mistresses mother."

The corners of Jamie's mouth tightened. "No, but then I never brought another woman into the house before, either. What do you expect me to do—sneak in and out of your bedroom in the middle of the night? Or are you expecting me to set you up in a love nest at the other end of town and see you on Wednesdays and weekends? As I remember, perhaps that's more your style, isn't it?"

Their conversation was taking a predictable, ugly turn. She should have known they could not talk to each other—they could not do anything together, except make love. Both of them knew this, yet neither could summon the strength to walk away. How long their relationship could survive the strain, she had no idea. If only she could talk to him. It should be easier now to explain that Stash was the half-brother Stan that she had often talked about, but whom he had never met. But his present attitude made it impossible for her to bring the subject up.

"I . . . I just don't want to . . . to do anything to hurt Cal," she defended herself.

"I don't think it would hurt him to know that his mother and father sleep together," he said bluntly.

"He might expect it to lead to something more . . . more permanent," she blurted, "and you did warn me not to—"

"I've changed my mind." He clipped the words. "Whatever happens between us, you'll always be Cal's mother and I'll never do anything to keep you two apart. The boy needs to call you mother as much as I need to call you Manya," he added in a hoarse whisper.

Without thinking she flew into his arms. "Oh, Jamie, thank you. You don't know how much that means to me."

His arms went around her, completing the embrace. "Does it mean that you'll move your things into my room?" he teased.

If only it were that simple. Even locked in his

arms she did not have the courage to tell him how much she feared and resented Barbara's influence in his life; how this ever-present specter of his infidelity pained her. Mary was confident now that his affair with Barbara was definitely over; still, she was definitely a taboo subject. Her role as Jaycie's mother had given her privileged status in Jamie's eyes that Mary was not allowed to question.

"I just don't want to live in that house," she choked.

"We *have* to live there," he said with infuriating logic, "if I'm to run for election in Jackson County. Our other house is across the state line in Johnson County, and I'd be a Kansas resident instead of a Missourian."

"I'd forgotten," she admitted in a small voice. "But couldn't we find another house in Jackson County?"

"After the election, I'll look," he promised, adding, almost as an afterthought, "if we're still together," so that she knew that he, too, was wondering how long the magic between them would last.

"It's settled, then." A statement, not a question. And since she was not called upon to answer, she merely burrowed her head deeper into his shoulder and prayed that it was.

The long ride back to Kansas City was driven in deep silence. Not the angry silence of their trip out, for Jamie kept her firmly anchored to his side, with his right arm tight around her shoulders so that a companionable warmth flowed back and forth between their bodies, but a silence nevertheless. He was deep into thoughts of the coming campaign, she told herself, while her own thoughts were a jumble of fears and apprehensions that magnified as they neared their destination.

The many reasons why they were chained to Fitzhugh's house kept sifting through her consciousness. Jamie needed its address for a political base and he needed to live there to prevent his father from evicting Barbara, and thereby, Jaycie. If she wanted to live there with him and Cal, she would have to accept this. But could she? Nothing had really changed since that day over four years ago when she had run away from this same situation.

How could he expect her to forget the past if his former mistress continued to live in the same house with them? No woman should be expected to live under those conditions, and he had no right to ask it of her. A shudder of despair ran through her body, and to her dismay, the tears that she had brushed back with her eyelashes started to squeeze their way past that barrier and down her cheeks.

Immediately Jamie drew the car off to the side of the road and parked it. "What is it now?" he demanded, his voice impatient, yet rough with worry as he tried to peer down into her averted face.

Mary wanted to turn into his arms and forget the horrid thoughts and jealousies that were plaguing her, but she could not forget them. There simply was no future for them, or—as he preferred to say—no present. The wounds were too deep.

"It was too perfect to last," she sobbed, remembering the feel of his arms around her, the ecstasy of her surrenders to him.

"It still is," he soothed, uneasy at the note of desperation in her voice and note of finality in the way she tried to draw away from him.

"I just can't," she blurted out. "I want to, so much. But I can't."

"Don't cry, honey." He dabbed her tears away with clumsy fingers. "Of course you don't have to do anything you don't want to." He kissed away the moisture that his fingers had not been successful in mopping up. "Exactly what is it that you can't do?" He was so sure of what they had that he could not believe he had heard her reply correctly.

"I can't live with you in that house." She twisted her face away, not wanting the comfort that he was offering because it was weakening her resolve. His body stiffened against hers in disbelief.

"I thought it was all decided." His voice was cold with shock.

"I want to be with you," she assured him between sobs. "I haven't changed my mind about that. But not in that house." There was so much more that she wanted to say, but the words refused to come. In all these years she had never been able to discuss Barbara's role in his life, and she could not find the courage to do so now. Oh, God, why couldn't she stop this sniveling and discuss the matter with him rationally?

"Then where?" he said curtly, his arms dropping from her shoulders, leaving her cold and lost as he put her away from him.

"May—maybe an apartment of my own wouldn't be such a bad idea," she suggested diffidently. "You could come there whenever you wanted."

"And exactly what do you think that would do to the myth of the happily reconciled Fitzhughs?" he spat out.

"I don't know," she admitted in a small voice. "I'm just so confused."

"What is it, Manya?" he growled. "Do you want to have your cake and eat it, too? Do you want a house of your own so that you can entertain me, and then your other boyfriends on the nights I don't come?"

Her face went white with shock. So he still thought that of her. She wiped her tears away with an angry swipe of the back of her hand. "I'm not like that. I thought I had convinced you of that at least. I know I've made you angry, but I just don't know what to do, and we keep getting nearer and nearer to . . . to the house."

Mary could see the great effort he made to control his anger. "Okay, that was a rotten thing to say, and I'm sorry. I'm trying to understand you, Manya." A thin edge of irritation rasped his voice. "But you're not making much sense. You have to admit that. If you could only tell me what's really bothering you. I can't believe it's Fitz's house. It's only an inanimate object, for God's sake!''

Jamie put a gentle finger to her chin and tilted her face up to him. "I'm not starting this car again until you tell me the real reason you dread going back. Is it someone in the house? Has someone there hurt you in some way? Just tell me about it, and I promise I'll make it right."

An almost imperceptible flicker in the depths of her eyes convinced him he was on the right track. "It *is* someone in the house," he stated triumphantly. "Was it Fitz? He's a rough-speaking old rascal, I know, but he wouldn't deliberately hurt your feelings. He wants us to reconcile; he's told me so many times."

"No," she gulped, "not Fitz."

"But someone?" he persisted.

"I don't want to talk about it." She brushed his hand away in a wild gesture. "I just don't want to live with you in that house. Why can't you accept that?"

"Because I can't accept not knowing what's bothering you. Don't you understand?" His voice was a husky whisper. "Your happiness is important to me. You can't expect me to ignore something that is upsetting you like this. You might as well save time and tell me, because I'm not letting the matter drop if we have to sit here all night." His hand reached out again to cup her chin while his iron-flecked eyes tried to peer deep into her very soul. "Talk to me, Manya," he entreated.

It was the look in his eyes that was her undoing. Something in their dark, smoky depths reached out to her, convincing her that it was time to forget her past inhibitions and confide in him. With a sudden clarity she realized that he wanted their relationship to continue as much as she did. Surely, when he knew how important it was to her, he would let Barbara go. Mary was frightened; more frightened than she had ever been in her life, but she knew that if she did not make the attempt now, she never would.

Ever so cautiously, trusting him for the first time in four years, she let her guard down just the littlest bit.

"Wh-what if I a-asked you to send Barbara away?" She forced the words past reluctant lips. "W-would you do it?"

His body stiffened and his face became that bland stranger's mask she knew so well. "What has Barbara to do with us? Surely you're not jealous of her," he sneered. "She's just the housekeeper—nothing more—and a damn good one. You can't expect me to throw her out, just like that. Where would she go? What would she do? She's been with us for years. And there's Jaycie to consider. Ask me anything else," he pleaded.

The pain of his refusal was almost more than she could bear. She felt like a boxer who had come to the middle of the ring to shake hands and had been dealt a punch to the jaw instead. Her head reeled.

"Then, you wouldn't—let her go, that is." She finished the thought aloud, more for her benefit than his, then turned away to look out the window. How could she have been stupid enough to put the matter into words and reveal her own vulnerability?

"Don't do that," he snapped, his fingers reaching out to turn her face back toward him. "Don't you dare turn away from me and shut me out. We're done with that—you and I!"

Obediently she turned back to face him, but her blue eyes were bruised and shuttered as she met his gaze. Her hands rested nervelessly in her lap.

"Damn you, Manya," he grated, "why do you always have to look so vulnerable, and why do you have to ask me for the one thing I can't give you?"

Her lips grew stiff with the effort of trying not to droop and her eyes ached from holding back the tears that she had forbidden to surface, but she said nothing. Somewhere deep inside the brightly burning flame she had been coaxing to life over the past week sputtered and went out. She felt cold and empty and alone.

In the back of her mind she had always known that she could not win if she asked Jamie to choose between her and Barbara. Perhaps that was why she had never put her hopes into words before. It had been that idiotic look in his eyes, which she had mistaken for genuine concern, that had betrayed her. She would not be so gullible again.

"I can't explain without involving a lot of other people." His voice penetrated the numbness that was engulfing her. "But I can't possibly send Barbara away just now. She'd take Jaycie with her, and I don't want that to happen."

"Jaycie means a good deal to you, I know," she heard herself answer politely.

"She means more to me than anything in the world except Cal, and—" he hesitated—"and she needs me even more than Cal does. Cal, at least, has you and Fitz who love him, too. I can't let her down by sending Barbara away."

"No, I guess you can't," she agreed in a dull voice. In a perverse way she could almost admire him for standing by his daughter, but it did not ease the misery she felt.

"I don't give a damn about Barbara. You realize that, don't you?" he insisted. "If I thought for a minute she would go and leave Jaycie behind, I wouldn't hesitate to get rid of her. You've no reason to be jealous of her. Believe me."

Her face flamed. Jealous, was she? Well, even if it were true, she would die before admitting it and giving him another weapon to hold over her.

"Don't be a conceited ass," she sputtered. "Why should I be jealous of any of your women?"

"She's not one of 'my women,' as you call them," he explained wearily. The questioning tilt of her eyebrow made him hasten to add, "I told you, I don't have any women at all right now. Except for you. I *do* still have you, don't I?" he asked in a strained voice.

Did he? She wasn't sure. She couldn't let him go and she couldn't accept him as he was. The specter of Barbara continued to stand between them.

"I think," she said, speaking very slowly, trying

to sort out the words before she uttered them, "I think that when we get back to your father's house, we shouldn't rush into anything we'll regret. I'll take my old suite of rooms for the present, and you should do the same. Your political friends will continue to think we're a happily married couple, and we—we can take a little more time to decide exactly what we are."

"No, damn it," he thundered, "I don't intend to sneak around my own house in the dead of night to sleep with my own wife."

She forced a half smile. "It's not your house and I'm not your wife, remember? I'm your mistress. And perhaps when we get there, I won't even be that."

For a moment she thought the fingers clasping her shoulders so tightly would move up to her throat and strangle her. "I'm sorry, Jamie"—she tried to soften the shock she had given him—"but the decisions we made when there were just the two of us to consider suddenly seem much more complicated now that others are involved. I can't allow your father or Cal, or even Barbara and Jaycie, to believe we have completely reconciled when we both know that this is only a temporary situation."

"I don't give a damn about the others. This just concerns you and me—and perhaps Cal," he gritted, "and he certainly can't be hurt if he thinks we're back together."

"While we live in that house," she corrected him, "what we do is the business of everyone else who lives there."

"All right. I'll get us a house of our own as soon as I can," he promised. "Will that satisfy you?" He tried again to draw her into the circle of his arms. "I'll get you anything you want," he groaned against her throat. Then, realizing what he had said, he gave a mocking laugh to ease the seriousness of his words. "I'm very generous to my mistresses."

He had not meant to be cruel, just flip, but the taunt struck a nerve. How many mistresses had there been before her? How many would follow after? She must be insane to involve herself with him again. If only he would stop touching her, perhaps she could think more clearly. She pulled out of his arms and held her voice steady. "When we do have a house of our own, that's when I'll live with you openly."

"Getting a house will take some time," he said evasively, "and I don't want to wait. There are things to be considered you don't know anything about."

"But I do," she corrected him with a bitter smile. "Your father told me all about Jaycie."

He could at least be embarrassed to have the matter out in the open; instead, he seemed relieved that she knew. "Then you understand why I just can't ask Barb to go right now; or why I can't move us to another place without first making sure she doesn't disappear with Jaycie."

"Yes, Jaycie needs you, doesn't she?" She wanted to scream that she needed him, too, but she kept her voice cool and steady. If it didn't bother him to talk about his illegitimate daughter, she would not let him see how much it bothered her.

"She's such a great kid," he said, his face lighting up with pleasure just thinking of her. "It's not her fault she's caught up in grown-up squabbling. I have to help her every way I can, even though I know that Barb is just using her as a pawn to get money out of the family."

"And very successfully, it would seem." Mary could not prevent the snide remark from slipping out. "Fitz told me about the trust fund you've already set up for Jaycie, and he seems to think it won't be too long before you set up a similar trust for Barbara as well." She was amazed that she could discuss so dispassionately a subject that was tearing her apart internally.

Jamie thrust an impatient hand to the back of his neck. "I know what Dad thinks. He's being completely unreasonable about Barb and he's taking it out on Jaycie as well. I've tried to convince him that we can't allow Jaycie to suffer because we know Barb is greedy, but he's a stubborn old man."

He gave her a quick, appraising look. "Is that what this is all about? Has Fitz talked you into helping him get rid of them? You resent Jaycie for the circumstances of her birth, too, don't you? I thought you were fond of the kid, but you're as bad as the old man. No doubt he's convinced you that Cal's inheritance is in danger. Why can't the both of you realize that we have a duty to Jaycie and there's plenty for the two of them to share?" He gave her a disgusted look. "Or perhaps you're afraid I might be less generous with you as a result of helping her?''

The scorn in his voice infuriated her. How dare he. He was the one who had fathered an illegitimate child; and now, instead of at least being ashamed of it, he was trying to make her feel guilty. And in typical Fitzhugh fashion he had reduced the argument to a matter of money. Well, he could have his precious Barbara, his precious Jaycie, and most of all, his precious money.

"I would not live with you now if you bought me a castle," she hissed through clenched teeth. "I will return with you to Fitz's house and I will stay there until after the election, because I promised Cal that I would; but immediately after that, I am moving out. And while I am living under the same roof with you, don't you dare lay one finger on me."

Mary reached up with trembling fingers and tried to undo the gold chain from around her neck, but in her agitated state the clasp proved too illusive for her clumsy fingers. "Damn," she cried in exasperation.

He watched incredulously while she struggled to work the clasp free. Finally her fingers obeyed her and she held the necklace out to him. "Take it," she insisted.

His eyes darkened like a tornado funnel cloud. "Put that back on, Manya," he threatened in a menacing growl. "*Now*," he roared.

She jumped in her seat at the angry tone of voice that unexpectedly erupted from him, and some primitive instinct for survival advised her to do exactly as he said. Meekly she refastened the chain around her neck, lowering her eyes from the fury in his to stare timidly down into her lap.

His eyes glittered as he watched her obey his taut command, then, with a snort of rage, he turned away from her and restarted the car. It jumped back onto the highway with a jerk as he pressed the accelerator down to the floor. The speedometer began to climb and she paled.

"You're...not going to...speed again?" She quavered, terrified of him in this black mood.

Jamie stared straight ahead at the road, only the tightness of his hands on the wheel revealing the strain he was under. "Just be very quiet," he told her with a disarming softness that only accentuated his fury. "Don't say another word. Don't move. Don't even think. If you are very, very still, I just might change my mind and not drive us both off the next bridge!"

Chapter Eleven

Cal knew something was wrong the moment the car came to a halt in an angry squeal of brakes in front of the massive stone front entrance. He had been watching the car's approach along the circular drive, and when he was sure that it was his father, he started running across the wide expanse of green lawn at an angle that would intercept it when it came to a halt.

"I was watching for you," he shouted, out of breath, as he slammed to a stop against the parked car. "I missed you, Dad. I missed you, too, Manya."

He tugged at the handle of the front door with impatient fingers that were stilled the moment he had a good look at his father's dark, furious face. His smile faded. Casting a worried look from one to the other of the car's occupants, his faded smile was replaced with a perplexed frown.

It was obvious that his father was in one of his black moods; and while Manya seemed all right, the corners of her mouth were pinched in a tight line and her eyes looked sad. He hoped that Dad had not been angry with her. He had known the coldness of his father's anger on rare occasions and he did not like to think of Manya having to face it. She was only a girl, after all, and would not understand that sometimes when Dad was in a bad mood, he said things that he did not really mean. At such times Cal had learned it was best to speak only when spoken to and soon enough Dad would be over his anger.

It was mostly since Manya had come to live with them that Dad had these dark moods. Cal felt disloyal even thinking this and he promised himself that he would have a talk with her sometime soon about the best ways to handle Dad. In the meantime he made an effort to comfort her.

"Are you all right, Manya?" His whispered words were meant for her ears only; but unfortunately for him, his father overheard and for some reason was angered even more.

"Your mother is fine, Cal," he answered for Mary in a reproving voice that got Cal's attention immediately. "And see that you call her that from now on. You don't call me Jamie, and you are not to call her Manya. Do you think you can remember that?"

"S-sure, Dad. But I thought you didn't want me to—to—you know." He reddened in embarrassment.

His father's thundercloud face grew even more ominous. "No, Cal, I don't know. I've never forbidden you to call her mother, have I?"

A simple "No, sir" was called for here, but Cal

was too bewildered to be cautious. "But, Dad, didn't Barbara say that if she wasn't staying, I should not start calling her—"

"This does not concern Barbara," his father thundered, his hand coming down heavily on Cal's slight shoulder in emphasis, "and you are not to discuss your mother or me with Barbara at any time. Do you understand that?"

The "Yes, sir" came automatically this time, through stiff lips, as Cal wondered what it was he had done wrong now. His father would never strike him, he knew that, but the heavy pressure of that hand on his shoulder gave him a sick feeling in the pit of his stomach.

He stood there in misery, wondering what to do next, when he watched with disbelief as his mother's small, scarred hand came to rest admonishingly over his father's huge bronzed paw where it rested a moment before gently lifting it from Cal's shoulder. "You're frightening him," she chided bravely.

Cal looked at the two of them with trepidation. He understood that in her own way she was trying to help him, but he feared for her safety now. He had not had time to warn her that it was dangerous to interfere when Dad was in a temper. He held his breath, waiting for the explosion that should have come.

To his amazement, instead of brushing that interfering hand away, his father folded it carefully into his and just stood there holding it and looking at his mother with a funny expression on his face. It was suddenly apparent to Cal that for some unfathomable reason Dad wasn't angry at anyone anymore.

To further emphasize this metamorphosis, his father's other hand was now roughing up Cal's hair. "Don't mind me, Son. You've got a grouch for an old man. Luckily your mom's here now to take the rough edges off. She'll have us both purring like kittens from now on, and about time, too, I would guess. We've needed a woman's soft touch around here for a long time now."

Cal could have reminded him that there were lots of women around the house—Barbara, Millie, Cook, and the others, but somehow even he knew that was not what his father was talking about. They were a family now, with a gentle mother who was allowed to beard the lion in his den, and declaw him when necessary; and judging from the bemused look on his father's face, the lion was pleased to have it that way. He looked up at his father, and the two of them exchanged conspiratorial grins.

"Why don't you take your mom's small case up to my room," his father suggested, looking over his son's head at Mary, who stared back at him in indignant surprise. Their eyes battled silently for a long moment, and his grip on her hand tightened.

For the first time since he could remember Cal did not move immediately to obey his father, but waited warily for a signal from the woman who had subdued his father with a touch of her hand.

Tugging free of Jamie's grip, Mary knelt beside her son. Did she have any choice in the matter? Yet a touch of her old spirit urged her to say

"You're not to take that case anywhere!" Then with an impudent face to the now glowering lion, she added with a laugh, "Until you give your mother a big hello kiss!"

It was too good to be true. "Mom. Oh, Mom." Cal threw himself into her arms, hugging her fiercely.

Above them, Jamie's tight smile relaxed into one of satisfaction tinged with relief. Regardless of what she said, there was no way Manya would leave him or Cal now. He found himself kneeling beside the two of them, wrapping a protective arm around each, as though by sheer physical force he could hold this newly formed family together against the outside world.

That was the tableau that met Barbara's eyes when she threw open the front door. She, too, had watched the car approach the house and wondered what was keeping them. The picture before her was most annoying. A family reunion was not at all in her plans for the future. She covered her displeasure with a brisk air of efficiency.

"Here, Cal, give me that bag." She reached down to take the small suitcase standing on the curb beside him.

"No, no," he shouted, breaking loose from his parents and picking up the bag before Barbara could take it from him. "Dad wants me to take Mom's bag to his room," and he scooted off as though he were afraid she would take the honor away from him.

"Your room?" The questioning lilt in Barbara's voice as she looked sharply at Jamie indicated that there must surely be a misunderstanding, and she waited patiently for the explanation.

It was the moment that Mary had been dreading, the reason for their fight in the car. Only the remembered warmth of her son's arms around her kept her from turning and running away. She rose slowly, helped by Jamie's supporting arm around her waist.

"Have someone see that the rest of my wife's things are moved to the master suite immediately," he commanded, instead of explaining.

"B-but—" Barbara started to protest; however, he had already turned back to Mary and was leading her into the house. In the entrance way he turned back as another thought came to him.

"Oh. I almost forgot. In the trunk of the car you'll find all those clothes that came from Adler's. None of them were suitable, after all. Please see that they are returned and credited to my account."

This was another thing she had not planned on. In the back of her mind she had entirely different plans for those clothes when Mary rejected them, as she never doubted she would. "I don't think the store will take them back, Jamie," she explained sweetly. "After all, they weren't purchased on a trial basis."

He shot her a shrewd glance. "In that case," he countered smoothly, "call my secretary and explain the details to her. I'm sure she'll be able to come to some arrangement with the store. She's quite a formidable old dragon."

Mary did not miss the look of pure venom that

Barbara cast in her direction before she hurried off to get help for the rest of the luggage; however, taking a deep breath, she tried to dismiss the episode from her mind.

"So, Miss McQueen is still with you after all this time," she said instead with a remembering smile. "I recognized the description."

He returned her smile, sharing an old memory with her. "Yes, Queenie still runs the office and me with it." He peered closely at Mary, trying to gauge her mood. She seemed more relaxed—not tense and frightened as she had been in the car. His own anger had dissipated as soon as she had placed her hand on his. She had only to touch him...

"You're staring at me," she said.

"I was wondering if our fight was over," he mused as he hooked one finger under the gold chain around her neck with the pretense of adjusting it and allowed his other fingers to brush the soft warm skin beneath.

She gave a deep, despairing sigh. "Yes, I suppose it is. But only because you seem to have gotten your own way, as usual."

It was true and he was very pleased with himself. She was here in this house and she would be sharing his room, his bed. He could not control the grin of triumph that tugged at his lips.

"It's not official until we kiss and make up," he informed her solemnly, pulling at the chain to draw her closer so that he could bend down to claim her mouth.

Her lips moved and parted for him, giving him

the access he wanted, and her arms slipped around his waist as he folded her into his arms. They held each other until, reluctantly, he raised his head. "I can't let you have your way," he groaned against her forehead, "because you want to do crazy things like leave me; and I can't permit that. You belong to me again and I'll never let you go."

She tipped her head up and gave him an impudent look. "I thought we were only going to have a casual affair; one that either of us could walk away from at any time."

"You and I are going to have an affair," he agreed shamelessly. "It's Cal's mother that I won't permit to leave. I'll kill her if she tries to go," he groaned.

The intensity of this declaration shook her to the very core of her being, echoing as it did her own unspoken thoughts. Since they had quarreled so violently in the car, the tension between them had been building up to this point of no return. No matter that he had his reasons for hating her and she had her reasons for hating him; that hatred was as puny as the flare of a single match compared to the forest fire of passion that was consuming them. There was no way either of them could walk away while that fire burned. At last she accepted this and tightened her hold around his waist, burying her flushed face into his chest.

"Never, never let me go," she whispered into his coat. "This is where I belong."

He sank into a chair and pulled her down onto his lap. His hand splayed itself across her heaving breast, cupping it through the thin material of her dress until the nipple rose taut under his thumb. He started to fumble with the buttons at the back of her dress when a nervous cough interrupted him.

Angrily he looked around to see Barbara standing in the doorway, holding an excited Jaycie firmly in front of her. Embarrassed, Mary tried to rise, but Jamie kept her firmly anchored on his lap. "A very good reason for getting a house of our own, soon," he grumbled into her ear.

The face that he turned to Barbara mirrored his annoyance. "Perhaps you might get in the habit of knocking before entering a room you know is occupied," he suggested with chilling politeness.

Barbara blanched but held her ground. "The door was partly open," she choked, "and Jaycie was anxious to see you." She threw Mary a spiteful glance. *This is my trump card,* her eyes said eloquently, *and I'm playing it now.*

The sight of the little girl straining to see her father was like a physical blow to Mary. She had no weapon against such innocent adoration. The child wanted Jamie's love and attention and, in spite of her mother, she was entitled to it. She tried again to rise from Jamie's lap, intent on leaving the room so that he might have some time alone with his daughter, but he held her firmly in place.

Meanwhile Jaycie squirmed free of her mother's hold and ran across the room to clutch at Jamie's arm. "I missed you, Jamie," she chattered, and then stopped, staring with indignation at Mary. "There's no room for me," she wailed, seeing her favorite spot usurped.

Jamie gave an indulgent laugh. "Sure there is, cupcake." With a deft movement he transferred Mary's weight to one knee and hoisted Jaycie up on the other. "There's plenty of room for both my girls."

Again Mary tried to wriggle free. "I really have things to do," she pleaded mendaciously into his ear.

"Later," he commanded gruffly.

Jaycie looked from one face to the other with a child's curiosity and just a hint of pique. "Is Mary your best girl now, Jamie?" Her lower lip quivered. "Cal says she is. He says she's his mother, too. Now you and Cal won't like me anymore."

"Nonsense." He gave her sandy curls a reproving tug. "Now I have two best girls—a little one and a grown-up one; and you have another person who is going to like you very much. Someone who helped me buy a little present for you, as a matter of fact," he added in a conspiratorial tone.

"A present? Really?" Her eyes shone. "I knew you wouldn't forget," she confessed artlessly. "What did you buy me? What? What?"

"I suppose I won't have a minute's peace until I show you, will I? Well, come on, cupcake." He took his two best girls by the hand and stood, drawing them up with him. "Let's go to my room and search for it."

Barbara stood, forgotten, in the doorway, glowering at them. Mary's quiet acceptance of Jaycie's

presence had not been what she expected. She
had hoped that her daughter would have an abrasive effect on the moonstruck couple, but apparently it was not to be. She struggled to contain her
frown.

Looking up, Jamie seemed surprised that she
was still standing there. He dismissed her with a
nod. "See that dinner's ready in an hour, would
you? And, Barb, ask Fitz to join us."

She nodded pleasantly while fuming inwardly.
Being dismissed like an ordinary servant was bad
enough, but the reference to Fitz put her on notice that Jaycie would not be expected to join them
for dinner—Fitz did not allow it. She turned and
left the room in a huff.

Although the older woman had not once glanced
in her direction, Mary felt her hatred. With a
shiver she looked over at Jamie, but he was blissfully unaware of the tension and she vowed to
take a leaf from his book. As long as Jamie was by
her side, there was no way that Barbara could hurt
her any longer. She had done her worst, destroy-
ing Mary's life for the past four years, but Mary
was determined now not to let the past hurt her
again. As Jamie said, from now on they would live
in the present—one day at a time.

In defiance of her past fears, she slipped free of
Jamie's restraining hand. He gave her a surprised,
wary look at this action, but when she moved to
the other side of Jaycie and took the child's free
hand, the smile that softened his features flooded
her with warmth.

"You are one fantastic lady," he told her as the

two of them swung the excited child between them. She glowed under his compliment, with only the hint of a smile to reveal how deeply gratified she was to have pleased him.

In the bedroom they found one of the maids making quick work of emptying her large suitcase, while another was moving her few possessions into the bureau drawers that had been emptied for her. Cal was sitting cross-legged in the middle of the bed, surrounded by clothes and packages, hugging the small suitcase in his lap. When he saw the three of them coming toward him, he jumped off the bed and ran to Jaycie, pulling her free of the adults.

"I told you," he whispered into her ear. "She is too my mom now. And this is her little suitcase." He held it out proudly but wouldn't let go of it. "I'm taking care of it for her. Isn't that right... Mom?" He turned wide expectant eyes toward Mary for confirmation.

It was the very innocence of his question that rebuked her, showing her clearly what she had deprived him of all these years. She had been so wrapped up in her own suffering that she had lost sight of the fact that she was not the only one affected by her decision to leave Jamie. Oh, Mary had accepted that her actions had punished Jamie and had punished herself, but for the first time she was realizing how much she had punished Cal as well.

During those awful four years she had missed Cal terribly, but even that had been in a selfish way—thinking of how empty her life was without him—never stopping to realize that his life, too, had lacked something because of her absence.

In her mind's eye she had always pictured him as being happy and contented—the rich little boy with an indulgent, loving father to see to all his needs—a boy who lacked neither material possessions nor love. And yet, the innocence with which he now stared at her told her how wrong she had been. With all that he had, there had still been an emptiness that only his mother could fill.

Now, looking up at her expectantly, he was not just asking her if he could hold her suitcase, he was asking her for how long. He was asking for confirmation that she was indeed going to be part of his life from now on.

Mary looked over his head at Jamie with repentant, guilt-stricken eyes. *I never realized,* she told him mutely. He gave her a mocking, soul-searching glance in return that asked her what she was going to do about it now that she knew.

In answer, she reached down and took Cal's hand in hers. "Thank you for taking care of my case, Cal, but why don't you give it to Millie now and she can unpack it for me. That is, if you really want me to stay." She laughed shakily, promising herself that nothing—*nothing*—would ever make her walk out of her son's life again.

"Do I!" he agreed, and to prove the point he handed the case to the waiting Millie. Now that he realized that his mother was really staying, he didn't need it any longer.

When he had divested himself of the suitcase, his father gave him a teasing grin and suggested that he might be interested in searching for some presents that seemed to have been misplaced somewhere in the jumbled mess on the bed. Drawing Mary to one side, the two of them watched as the children made short work of the search to come up with two suspiciously present-like packages. When a nod from Jamie indicated that they were on the right track, they ripped off the wrappings with a vengeance.

There was a picture book for Jaycie and a Monopoly game for Cal, which they solemnly promised to teach him to play that very evening after supper. At the same time they assured Jaycie there would certainly be time for a story from her new book before she went to bed. Then the children were shooed off to get ready for the evening meal.

Mary walked over to the bed and idly tried to bring some semblance of order to the mess that the children had made of its contents. She sensed Jamie coming up behind her, but was nevertheless surprised when he gave her a gentle shove that sent her sprawling on the already cluttered bed. Immediately the hard length of his own body followed hers, its weight pinning her down.

Mary, very much aware that Millie and her helper were still working in the far corners of the room, tried to slide away from Jamie's amorous bear hug, rolling her eyes frantically to signal the maids' presence. With an impatient shake of his head he received the message.

"Finish that later, Millie," Jamie called over his shoulder, not releasing his hold on his wife. With a giggle, entirely foreign to her usually staid manner, the middle-aged maid scurried out of the room, taking the younger girl with her and carefully locking the door behind her.

With a small triumphant war whoop, Jamie straddled Mary's body with his knees. "I've got you where I want you now, me proud beauty," he taunted with a melodramatic leer and a twirl of an imaginary mustache. "Surrender your virtue, or out you go, into the snow."

"P-please, s-sir," she started to go along with his charade, but dissolved in a fit of giggles instead. "Oh, Jamie, did you see the look on Millie's face. Poor thing. Whatever must she be thinking?"

"She's thinking we're going to make love before dinner," he leered, "and she's right." His dark gray eyes were no longer laughing.

Mary wasn't laughing, either, but felt compelled to offer a weak protest. "We can't. Cal and your father will be waiting. And the bed—all these clothes—we'd make a mess."

"Let them wait," he decided arbitrarily, but he gave the cluttered bed a considered look. "The floor, then?" he suggested hopefully, the glowing fire in his eyes not to be denied. His lips pressed moist kisses along the column of her throat while his fingers busily slipped her panty hose down past unresistant silken thighs. "The ceiling? The bathtub, perhaps?" he continued crazily as his busy fingers undressed her.

With a long, shuddering sigh of surrender, her hands moved to the buttons of his shirt, slipping the garment from his shoulders and flinging it away. "The floor, then," she agreed as he removed the last of her clothing with impatient fingers and slid her naked body off the cluttered bed onto the thick plush pile of the carpeting.

He did not join her at once, but instead removed the remainder of his own clothing, so that his own desire was immediately apparent and demanding. Mary lay in a graceful heap where he had placed her, but he deliberately denied himself the pleasure of joining her while he stared for a few seconds longer at the vision she made with her boneless body lying like fluid pink marble on the dark carpeting, her honey-blond hair spread in wild fingers of silk, beckoning to him.

She was intensely aware of his scrutiny through half-closed lashes, and for the first time in her life she was glad she was beautiful, because she could see that it gave him pleasure. Then, with an impish grin, she gave a slow-motion, sensuous stretch that spread her arms and legs wide in all directions. With an oath his self-imposed control cracked, and he fell to the floor beside her and gathered her hungrily into his arms.

"You did that on purpose, you vixen," he muttered as he punished her mouth with rough kisses.

"Yes," she gasped when he finally allowed her to breathe again, his lips already roaming to her breasts. "I got tired of waiting while you admired the scenery."

"Admiring the scenery, was I?" he groaned. "Well, I'm about to demolish the scenery now."

He took small tugging nips at her erect nipples. "I'll have you begging for mercy yet!"

Her hands tightened in his hair. "I am begging," she said simply, the laughter erased from her eyes.

With a sigh of pleasure his body slid easily between her open thighs, a throbbing, incomplete entity, seeking to be made whole in her moist warmth. He shuddered as their two separate bodies became one, became complete in each other. In savage, primeval rhythm they rocked together, hearts touching, racing, pounding, robbing each other of breath with kisses that had no beginning and no end. "Manya, Manya." The words were torn from his swollen lips. "I love—"

Suddenly there was a frantic pounding and shouting at the other side of the locked bedroom door—a harsh reality forcing its way between them. A woman was screaming hysterically and the door shook under a thunderous assault against it.

"Jamie, Jamie, come quickly." The voice was barely recognizable as Barbara's. "Something terrible has happened to Fitz!"

Chapter Twelve

The ride to the hospital in the ambulance was a nightmare in slow motion. Fitz was alive, but just barely, his face tinged blue under the oxygen mask. The two paramedics who had answered the call did all the right things, quickly and efficiently, including starting a heart that had obviously stopped, but now they seemed to have exhausted their repertoire of things to do and could only hope that the hospital's more sophisticated equipment could be reached in time to complete the work they had started.

In answer to Barbara's frantic call, Jamie had pulled on a pair of jeans and run bare chested and barefoot down the hallway to his father's room to find Fitz unconscious on the floor.

"I came to call him for dinner," Barbara was sobbing. "When he didn't answer my knock, I walked in and found him . . . like that. He's dead, Jamie, dead!"

Jamie shook off her clutching hands. "Get a hold on yourself and call an ambulance. Then stay with the kids. Keep them out of here." He fell on his knees before his father's prostrate form and started to administer artificial respiration.

A few minutes later Mary entered the room, dressed in wrinkled slacks and a clashing blouse, which she had plucked uncaring from the jumble of clothes on the bed. Her hair was tied back with a rubber band, making her shocked eyes even more prominent in her pale face. Jamie was breathing into his father's mouth with slow, measured strokes.

Her offers to help were rejected with a negative movement of his head as he continued his labored breathing—in and out, in and out—forcing air into his father's lungs, expelling it. When she thought he could not possibly continue a moment longer, the paramedics arrived and took over.

At the emergency entrance to the hospital a horde of nurses and interns shoved Jamie and Mary aside so that they could get at the injured man. One of the nurses took a moment to shuttle the couple off to a cold, sterile waiting room and suggested they stay there out of the way until there was further word on Fitz's condition.

Mary sank into the nearest chair, but Jamie paced the small room, ticking off the seconds with each impatient step.

"Come, Jamie. Sit down."

He ignored the suggestion. "Dad is only sixty. He's never been sick a day in his life. Now he's fighting to survive."

"Come. Sit down," she repeated. "You can't help him by wearing yourself out. We all need your strength now."

He continued to pace. Mary looked around the room and then stood up and headed toward the door.

"Where are you going?" he demanded.

"To find you some coffee and something to eat. You've missed lunch and now dinner."

"I'm not hungry, damn it."

"I know," she soothed. "I'll be right back."

He watched her walk away with a half frown on his face. Would she never learn to do as she was told? Then he resumed his methodical measurement of the small room.

When she returned, it was with a tray containing a thermal coffee pot, two paper cups, little packets of sugar and dry creamer, and some soggy sandwiches on a plate. "The kitchen was closed, but I managed this much," she said triumphantly. "Have a sandwich. I think it's tuna fish." She sniffed it disdainfully. "Maybe not."

He seemed to have forgotten her presence. With an oath he sank into a chair at the other end of the waiting room and buried his head in his hands. She watched him with troubled eyes. Without his cloak of arrogance to shield him, he seemed very vulnerable. Like Fitz himself, she thought with a stab of fear—one moment a giant, king of the hill, and now, suddenly, helpless as a child, his very existence at the whim of fate.

That mustn't happen to Jamie. He was the rock to which they all clung now. It was unfair that he should have to carry that burden, but it was irrefutable. No, it would never do for that rock to crumble.

She put down the tray and walked over to stand beside him, one slim arm encircling his broad bent shoulders. At her touch he started to tremble, and her other arm went around him, holding him tightly to her, burying his face in her bosom. His shoulders were shaking now, and though no sound passed his lips, she felt her blouse dampen where his face rested against her. His arms went around her hips, holding on to her desperately, and she drew him even closer. Neither of them spoke. Minutes passed, and she felt her legs cramp from standing too long in the same position, but she dared not move.

Finally Jamie cleared his throat and moved his head slightly, tipping it up so that he could look at her with shamed, haggard eyes. "Well, so much for your tower of strength," he said derisively.

"You are," she insisted with vehemence. "You're the strongest man I know. It was a terrible shock, finding Fitz like that, but that didn't stop you from administering artificial respiration, which probably saved his life. You're entitled to a delayed reaction now."

"My champion," he mocked ruefully. "Who would have thought it?" Pain and self-derision were still strong in his eyes as he allowed his guard to remain down so that she could see and share his torment. Then, abruptly, he filed it away, but they both knew that he had allowed her, however briefly, into a very secret place.

Breaking the spell, he gave her a sharp tap on the derriere. "Give me one of your damn sandwiches now. It will probably be a long night."

They emptied the contents of the thermal coffee pot and refilled it and emptied it again before the doctor finally arrived with word of Fitz's condition. The sober-faced man was not encouraging. Fitz was rallying but was still in grave danger. He had had a massive heart attack, and if he did not have another one in the next twenty-four hours, he had a chance. In the meantime, since he was heavily sedated, the doctor suggested that the family go home for the night, since there was nothing they could do.

However, he had not reckoned with Jamie, who assured him with all of his usual arrogance that the family had no intention of going home. "I intend to stay here at the hospital until I'm sure Fitz is out of danger. I'd appreciate it if you could arrange a cot close by so that I'll be within call."

The doctor shook his head in defeat. "I'm too tired to argue with you, Mr. Fitzhugh; and after the last time, I know I'd only be wasting my breath. I'll have my nurse get the room you used last time ready for you."

Mary saw the tips of Jamie's ears turn a dull red as he walked the doctor to the door, out of earshot. When he returned, he was very brisk. "Take a cab home, Manya, and get some sleep."

She brushed his words aside. "What was the doctor talking about? When did you stay overnight in the hospital?"

The tips of his ears were red again. "When Cal broke his wrist, I think," he mumbled. "It was no big deal."

"When else?" she prompted, knowing the answer.

"I'm really tired, Manya. I'm going to find that room and sack out for a while." He attempted to brush past her, but her fingertips on his shoulder brought him to a halt.

"It was when I was sick, wasn't it?"

"You're turning into a nag, Mary." She knew he was annoyed, but she continued to block his path.

"Wasn't it?"

"Damn it, what if it was? Was I supposed to leave you there alone? You didn't have anyone else that cared."

"But you hated me so much," she mused. "Why should it have mattered to you? We'd been apart for four years."

"Because I..." He could not bring himself to say the words she wanted to hear. "Perhaps because I'm a fool," he blurted out angrily, his eyes heavily shuttered against her intrusion, refusing to allow her that final victory. But it was no good. He had shown her his secret place and now he had nowhere to hide from her.

Her arms moved slowly up his chest and around his neck as she stood on tiptoe to hug him tightly to her. She *knew*, whether he wanted her to or not. "I know," she murmured, "so am I."

Then, because this was not the time nor the place to pursue the matter, she stepped back. "I'd better go home and see what's happening there. I'll be back later this morning. Can I bring you something?"

"Don't come back before noon," he growled.

"All right," she agreed meekly, reaching up to kiss him softly on the lips once more before she turned and walked away.

He watched the soft sway of her hips until the elevator doors closed behind her. Stubborn woman. She'd be back whenever she damn well pleased. He licked his lips to taste her kiss again.

It was four o'clock in the morning when Mary went to bed, and she set the alarm for eight. When it went off, she was already in the shower. Despite all that had happened, she was humming to herself. She came out of the bathroom, wrapped in Jamie's robe, which had been hanging behind the door. Still fussing with the belt, she looked up to see Cal, fully dressed, sitting on the edge of the bed, stale tears staining his cheeks.

"Is Grandpa going to die?"

She wrapped her arms around him. "I don't know, Cal. I hope not, but he is very, very sick. Your father's with him now."

He took courage from that. "Dad won't let anything happen to him."

She smoothed his hair back. "Oh, Cal. Your father is only a man. God decides who dies."

"But I don't want God to let Grandpa die," he insisted. She drew him down beside her on the rumpled bed and listened as he poured out his fears, trying to erase them as much as possible without giving him any false hope. Words were not much good, and mainly they held on to each other and drew comfort from that.

Later they went down to breakfast together, and she agreed that he would not have to go to school today, that he would be much more useful at home, taking care of Jaycie. As though on cue, they found the little girl waiting for them in the small breakfast nook.

"Fitz is sick," she explained happily. "That means I can have breakfast with you."

"You're a brat, Jaycie." Her former protector turned on her savagely. "Just for that, go into the kitchen and eat by yourself."

The innocent lower lip trembled. "Everybody's mad at me today. Even Mama. And Cook is crying in the kitchen."

Mary looked at her son and indicated that he should make amends. "She's only a baby. If you're going to keep her out of everyone's hair today, you'll have to do better than this. Now, will you see that she gets something to eat, or must I take care of it?"

Cal looked at his mother in surprise. In her own way, without raising her voice, she could be as formidable as his father. He gave a resigned shrug. "Come on, brat. We'll both go into the kitchen. Maybe Cook will let us have Pop-Tarts for breakfast."

Mary doubted that his wish would be granted, but watched them leave with relief. Worrying about Jaycie would help keep Cal's mind off Fitz. She walked over to the plugged-in coffeepot and poured herself a cup of coffee, noting absently with the first sip that it was a pleasant change from the bitter brew she and Jamie had been drinking last night. Immediately his drawn face came to mind, and she wondered if he had managed to get any sleep at all after she left.

Her thoughts were interrupted when Cook entered the room and silently slid a plate of scrambled eggs, bacon, and hot biscuits before her, along with a glass of iced grapefruit juice. Since this was normally one of the maid's duties, Mary knew that Cook had seized upon an excuse to get further word of Fitz. As gently as she could, she told the elderly woman what she knew.

Dabbing at the corners of her eyes with the edge of her apron, Cook turned to leave, and Mary pushed the plate of food away, anxious to be on her way. However, seeing this, Cook turned back to her and wagged an admonishing finger. "You just eat some of that, missy. You'll be needing your strength for what's ahead."

Almost her exact words to Jamie the night before. Choking back a sob, Mary nodded and reached determinedly for her fork. She had just managed to swallow a few bites when Barbara's malevolent voice made her look up.

"It must be marvelous to be so unfeeling, you can eat as though nothing were wrong!"

In spite of her resolve not to let the woman bother her, Mary lost her temper. "And you, of course, are all broken up," she snapped. However, a second look stunned her with the knowledge that Barbara was indeed distraught. She wondered why. Her brief affair with Fitz had been over for four years. Now there was open hostility between them and only a floundering servant-master relationship to replace their former closeness. "But you *do* care," Mary realized aloud.

"Yes, yes," Barbara admitted wildly. "I know I don't mean anything to him anymore, but why do you think I've swallowed my pride and stayed on these last four years? Taking his insults, his neglect. After all, he is the—" She stopped abruptly. When she spoke again, she had changed the subject. "What I came in about was the reporter. What do you want to do about him?"

Mary learned that a reporter had been camping on their doorstep since six that morning and refused to leave without talking to a member of the family. Mary's first impulse was to refuse to see him; however, she realized that he would only continue to hang around the house and might try to approach the children in her absence.

"Send him in." She sighed in resignation.

Robert Hooker could not believe his luck when he saw that it was young Mrs. Fitzhugh, herself, that he would be talking to. Nothing could have suited his purposes better. Old man Fitz was big news in the city, but other reporters from his paper were covering that story at the hospital; not that they would get much other than routine hospital bulletins with that hawk-eyed son of his at the scene.

The paper had sent him to the house, hoping that he might pick up some human interest angles from the servants. Mrs. Fitzhugh was a bonus indeed; especially since her mysterious bout with amnesia and subsequent reunion with her husband, who was big news in his own right since he had announced his candidacy for the vacant Congressional seat. There had to be a lot more to that story than had been printed so far, and it looked like he had been given an opportunity to find out. The pale young woman who was nervously facing him could prove to be a gold mine of information.

Mary held out her hand in greeting, and he shook it, glancing down as he did so at the scarred tissue that remained from her accident. Her eyes followed his, and he had the grace to flush.

"I didn't mean to stare. I met you when your husband took you home from the hospital. Your hands were heavily bandaged then. You seem to have recovered marvelously. In fact, you look great," he added admiringly, remembering the wan, terrified figure that had huddled in the backseat of the limousine that day.

"Thank you." She released her hand. "How can I help you now? Would you like some coffee?" Without waiting for an answer, she poured him a cup and set it down on the table beside her. "You're here about my father-in-law, I believe."

She was very friendly, in a most frustrating way. Although she seemed very forthright when he questioned her about Fitz—his career, his family, his past achievements—whenever he attempted to bring the conversation around to herself and her four years of amnesia, she would smile and remind him that since she couldn't remember anything about that period, there was nothing she could tell him, and anyway, Fitz was the person under discussion at the moment. He had not expected such polite but steely resistance to his forays into other areas of Fitzhugh life, especially from someone who had obviously never dealt with the press before. He could only assume that there really was nothing to tell. She was just a nice lady who had had amnesia and who was now very happily reunited with her family.

He decided to settle for that. Even without the sensational angle he had been hungering for, she was pretty enough to draw readers to any article that included her picture. "Perhaps I could take a photograph of you, Mrs. Fitzhugh," he suggested, mentally rewriting the story angle in his mind, "with your children."

He was too good a reporter to miss the apprehensive flicker in her eyes even though she answered calmly enough. "I have only one child, Mr. Hooker—my son, Cal. And I wouldn't like to draw public attention to him. It's distracting enough that his father and grandfather have to live in the public eye."

He frowned. "I could have sworn I saw two youngsters on the grounds earlier."

Carefully she took a long sip of her now-cold coffee. "The little girl is our housekeeper's daughter. She and Cal are company for each other."

Perhaps he might have let the matter drop at that, if the two children in question had not come skipping into the room. The boy—thin, wiry, with sand-colored curly hair and questioning gray eyes—was leading a small, chubby, apple-cheeked girl by the hand; the resemblance was remarkable. And didn't her husband have curly hair of the exact same shade as the two youngsters, and eyes of equally piercing gray? His reporter's antenna was quivering.

"How old is the little girl?" he asked casually.

Mary sat silently, trying to frame an answer, when Jaycie held up four fingers helpfully. "I'm going to be this many," she boasted.

"Oh, then she was born while you and Mr. Fitzhugh were separated," he observed. "What's her name?" He tried not to look too eager, but the trapped look in Mrs. Fitzhugh's eyes told him he was on to something.

"Jaycie Patterson," Mary stressed the last name softly.

"J.C." He thought about that a moment. "Like in James Calhoun," he joked, not joking at all.

"No. Like in J-a-y-c-i-e," Mary spelled out slowly. She rose from her chair. "Really, we're digressing, aren't we, Mr. Hooker? If you have no more questions, I really have to be getting to the hospital."

At that moment Barbara walked into the room. Her trim figure was lushly displayed in a blue silk dress and her auburn hair was piled high on her head. Her tears had dried and she had applied fresh makeup to her face. She looked regal and lovely. She cast a curious glance from the distraught Mary to the excited reporter. "I've come to get the children out of your hair," she explained in the tense silence.

Robert Hooker cast a surreptitious glance at her ringless left hand. "I'll just bet you're *Miss* Patterson," he announced triumphantly, and before either woman could say another word, he picked

up his hat. "Thanks for a very interesting interview, Mrs. Fitzhugh. I think you omitted one or
two important details our readers would be interested in, but I've no doubt that I can fill in any
blank spaces after I return to the office and re-
search the subject more thoroughly."

Mary sagged against the table. "He knows,"
she groaned, "and what he doesn't know, he'll
soon piece together. I've just ruined Jamie's career. I never should have let that man into the
house."

Barbara gave her a blank stare. "He seemed
nice enough to me, except for that crack about
being Miss Patterson. What on earth did you tell
him?"

Mary didn't have time for long explanations.
"He's figured out who Jaycie's father is and he's
bound to create a scandal. Don't talk to any more
reporters and don't let the staff talk to them,
either. And for God's sake, keep the children in
the house. Don't even let them walk around the
grounds. No doubt there'll be a photographer
with a telescopic lens here before long, trying to
get a picture of the two of them together."

Without further explanation she ran upstairs,
where she pulled out Jamie's overnighter and
packed a complete change of clothing for him,
along with a razor and other toiletries. Then she
hurried out of the house. She hoped Jamie had
been able to get some rest during the night, because she doubted he was going to get any the
remainder of this day.

At the hospital the downstairs lobby was swarming with reporters and to her horror she was instantly recognized. However, before they could reach her, two burly men in dark business suits hustled her into a waiting elevator, the small suitcase neatly tucked under the arms of one of the men.

"Just a minute," she protested.

"Mr. Fitzhugh's orders, ma'am. He doesn't want the press bothering you." She stifled a hysterical giggle. Where had they been earlier when she really needed them?

"Th-thank you, I think," she managed instead. "It was pretty frightening."

She expected that they would leave her when the elevator doors opened, but instead they walked her down the hall and into a small hospital room where one of the men deposited the overnighter on the floor. "Mr. Fitzhugh said you were to wait for him here. If you want something, we'll be right outside the door."

Before she could question them further, they had stepped out. She examined the small room curiously. The regulation hospital bed was messed, indicating that someone—Jamie, of course—had lain upon it. Other than that, it contained a small dresser, an overstuffed chair, and a bed stand. There was a door leading to an adjoining bath. She sank into the easy chair and wondered how she was going to tell Jamie what a botch she had made of the interview. He was so worried about his father, it seemed heartless to have to inflict this additional bad news on him, too, but he would have to know in order to protect himself. She clenched and unclenched her fists.

She had barely spared a thought for poor Fitz in all this. Now she wondered how he was doing. The security men had been very uncommunicative. Resolutely she rose and went to the door. Sure enough they were both still there, straddling straight-back chairs. They looked at her.

"Could one of you please find someone to tell me how Fitz is doing? And do you know where my husband is?"

They were reluctant to leave her door, but finally one was persuaded to go down the corridor to the nurses' station. The other told her that Jamie was with his father and would join her as soon as they had concluded their business.

"Business?" she squeaked. "What possible business could they have at a time like this?" However, no more information was forthcoming, so she reentered the room and waited again.

A few minutes later a nurse entered the room and assured her that Mr. Fitzhugh had had a comfortable night and, in fact, this morning he had insisted on sending for his lawyers, in spite of his doctor's objections, and was apparently still conducting some kind of a business deal.

"The man is at death's door," the nurse ranted. "He's on I.V., wearing an oxygen mask, and still he thinks he can conduct business as usual. Even tycoons can die, you know. He's doing himself more harm than good."

Despite the tirade, Mary sighed with relief. Apparently old Fitz was really every bit as tough as he appeared to be, or he wouldn't even be thinking about business. "And my husband? What is he doing?"

"Exactly what he pleases, it seems." The nurse shrugged resentfully. "Right now he and the other lawyers and a stenographer are all in with the patient. Dr. Amana is there, too, having an absolute fit over these goings-on."

The nurse's accurate summation of Jamie brought a trace of a smile to Mary's lips. "Has my husband had breakfast?" she said, trying to steer the conversation to calmer waters.

The nurse threw up her hands. "Not a thing. I brought him a tray and he practically threw it at me."

"He's so worried," Mary apologized for him. "Please don't judge him too harshly. Do you think it would be too much trouble to bring another tray?" She gave the nurse a despairing look. "He will be an absolute bear unless we can get him to eat something."

Despite her pique, the nurse laughed. "Men," she agreed and promised to have something sent in.

The new tray and Jamie arrived simultaneously. "What the hell is that?" he roared at the hapless candy striper who brought it in, deposited it on the bed stand, and left almost at a run. Mary shook her head reprovingly but said nothing as she poured the coffee and sweetened it the way Jamie liked it before handing it to him.

For the first time his haggard eyes recognized

her presence. She led him to the chair and settled him onto it, sinking beside him to sit on the footstool. He sipped the coffee. "I *told* you not to come back before noon."

"It's almost noon," she soothed, but an angry glance at his watch told him it was only ten.

"I can't go home," he growled. "Things are too unstable here."

"I brought you a change of clothes and a toothbrush." Idly she picked up a triangle of toast and handed it to him. He munched on it absently, his eyes watching the sunlight playing on her hair. When he finished it, she handed him another, and then a strip of bacon. When he realized what she was doing, he stopped eating.

"Damn it, Manya, you're feeding me like a baby," he complained.

"I know." Her lips curved. "I really don't mind, but as I remember from Cal, it was so much easier when the baby learned to use a knife and fork on his own. I think I'm going to have a problem getting the scrambled eggs to you this way."

He gave her hair a punishing tug for her impertinence and picked up the fork, making short work of the rest of the food on the tray while she sat silently watching. When he finished, he put the tray aside and pulled her onto his lap, giving her a warm, coffee-flavored kiss "for dessert." He grinned.

"I'm so glad Fitz is better," she sighed as she fitted herself against his chest. His arms tightened painfully around her.

"He's not. In fact, he's pretty bad, Manya." His voice broke. "I don't think he's going to make it."

She looked up at him in surprise. "But the nurse said he was well enough to have a business conference with his attorneys."

"I wish that were so. It was because he knows he doesn't have much time that he insisted on seeing his attorneys. He's adding a codicil to his will."

"Oh, Jamie." Her hands framed his face soothingly. "But surely a man like Fitz must have had his affairs in perfect order."

He shook his head. "Dad's will has needed changing for the past few years, but he's been too stubborn to admit it, until now. That's why I'm afraid it's the end. He wouldn't have taken care of it otherwise."

"But—"

He put a hand over her mouth. "I don't want to talk about it," he said harshly. "It was something he had to do and now it's done. You'll know about it soon enough."

"Of course," she agreed in a small voice, "I'm sure it doesn't concern me."

"You're right," he said curtly, "it doesn't." His words were cruel, but his arms were still around her. She remembered her own advice to the nurse and ignored his harshness. He had enough to worry about.

"How are the kids taking this? Have there been any reporters at the house? Perhaps I'd better send one of the men over there to keep them away."

"It's too late for that." She steeled herself for the explosion that was sure to come. "I've already talked to a reporter and— Oh, Jamie, I've probably ruined your career," she sobbed. "If only you had sent some men over earlier."

"What on earth are you talking about?" He turned her around to face him. "If I had sent a guard over, it would only have been to protect you. There's nothing you could say that could possibly hurt me or my career. Unless you told them about"—he gritted his teeth—"the man you were living with while we were separated."

Did he still think that? Surely she had explained about Stash. "No, no," she hastened to assure him. "It wasn't about me. He saw the...and when he looked at them... I just know he made the connection. He could hardly wait to get away and start checking further."

He gave her a gentle shaking. "What on earth are you talking about? What could he possibly see at the house that was so terrible?"

"The children," she sobbed. "He took one look at them together, and I could see he knew immediately that they were related. He's going to ruin you."

"Is that all?" He sighed in relief. "I wasn't sure you knew, that's why I never discussed it, but it will be common knowledge before long anyway. It's just something we'll have to live with, and eventually the newspapers will find something else to print."

"But—" She was confused that he could discuss it so calmly. "What about the committee?

Do you think they will still support you when they find out you have an illegitimate daughter?''

"What!" He stared at her in amazement, rising so quickly, she would have fallen if he had not held her. "Is that what you think?"

Now that it was out in the open, she could not bear to look at him. "I've come to terms with it," she mumbled miserably.

Two large hands cupped her face and forced her to look at him. The pain in her damp blue eyes was like a knife in his chest. "Sweetheart, sweetheart," he soothed huskily, impatiently, "I don't have an illegitimate child. Fitz does. Jaycie isn't my daughter—she's my sister!"

Chapter Thirteen

The room swirled dangerously around her. "B-but that's impossible." She sank weakly into the nearest chair, clutching the arms for support. Impossible. Impossible. Her words echoed and reechoed like a giant bell clanging in her head. Impossible. How could he lie to her about something like this just when she had begun to trust him again?

He wouldn't lie to her, she argued with the accusing inner voice; he wouldn't. And yet... The memory of Barbara's hysterical pronouncement four years ago could not be denied. Someone had lied to her, but who?

There was absolutely no reason for Barbara to lie. If Fitz were actually the child's father, Barbara would have been pleased to have such a hold over him and would have had nothing to gain by saying that it was Jamie's. Besides which, she and Barbara had been friends then, and she could have had no possible reason for wanting to break up her marriage.

As much as she wanted to believe differently, it had to be Jamie who was lying—perhaps because he thought the truth would shatter their new-found truce. He couldn't know that she had sworn to herself that nothing would ever make her leave him again. Yet, this very lie was causing her to question the wisdom of that vow. If only he had been man enough to admit what she already knew.

Mary broke free of his restraining arm and walked over to the window, keeping her back carefully to him so that he would not see the misery in her face. Once again words failed her and she could think of nothing to say to counteract this final, devastating betrayal on his part. Was that what their future was destined to be—a series of bland lies on Jamie's part whenever it suited his purpose? And if so, could she pay such a price? Was that what love was in the final analysis—enduring any humiliation to be with the object of your desire? She stared blindly out of the window and wondered if she could ever love strongly enough to be so weak.

Jamie came up behind her to take her shoulders between his hands and pulled her back against him. She tried to shake off the traitorous warmth that invaded her body whenever he touched her, but he would not allow it.

"Don't be like this, Manya," he persisted. "Surely you know I would not lie to you. There has never been anything between Barbara and me. Why, she was Dad's mistress at the time, and even if I hadn't been a deliriously happy man, which I was"—his lips touched the nape of her neck in gentle emphasis—"I certainly would not fool around with one of my father's women. At least credit me with that much discretion."

Why did he persist in prolonging this farce? Tears welled in her eyes. "It doesn't matter," she said in a small voice, "I told you that I had come to terms with it." It was not entirely true; she had accepted the facts, but not this final lie.

Angrily he swung her around to face him, "Well, damn it, I have not. And I don't intend to be forgiven by a sanctimonious little prig for something I never did!"

"Let's not go on with this!" He knew how she hated to argue, how she could never find the words to defend herself. She rubbed her moist eyes furiously with the back of her hand, disgusted with this further sign of weakness on her part. "Don't you understand? I'm not just guessing. I know!"

He gave her an impatient shove back into the chair. "You don't know anything," he disagreed vehemently, but any further explanation he might have given was interrupted by the appearance of a nurse in the doorway.

"Your father is asking for you, Mr. Fitzhugh."

Jamie looked from the nurse to Mary with suppressed fury. "I've got to go, Mary." He stared down at her with cold eyes. "There's no need for both of us to hang around here. Go back to the house and stay with Cal. We'll continue this discussion another time."

"But—"

"I said go home," he reiterated savagely, "and just to make sure you do as you're told, and to help keep those nosy reporters at bay, I'll send Max back with you."

"I don't want to leave," she protested, feeling that they could not let the matter remain unsettled.

"Why not?" he snapped, and she realized then the full extent of his fury. "Knowing what you believe me capable of, I'm surprised you can bear the sight of me at all."

Without giving her a chance to reply, he turned and followed the nurse out of the room, stopping briefly to whisper instructions to one of the two men on guard outside the door. Max, no doubt.

Her supposition proved correct when he left his partner and came over to introduce himself. Then, with a minimum of conversation, he dutifully escorted her home and promptly established himself as a buffer between Mary and the reporters and curiosity seekers who had gathered on the lawn of the mansion by promptly clearing a path for her through the throng in such a thorough manner that it did not allow room for argument on the part of anyone unfortunate enough to stand in his way. From then on he left her in no doubt that she now had a watchdog and protector.

If Mary wanted to leave the house, Max was instantly there at her side, carrying packages or blending into the background, but always there. It did not matter to him that she did not want to be chaperoned like some medieval Spanish virgin; he had his orders and he followed them to the letter. His constant presence was a disturbing reminder of her last angry conversation with Jamie and her isolated status from the rest of the world. Eventually she ceased leaving the house at all, rather than have him trail in silent disapproval behind her.

A week dragged by in this fashion. Many times Mary was tempted to confront Barbara with Jamie's amazing denial and have it out with her one last time, but as had always happened in the past, her pride would not allow her to do so. What defense would she have if Barbara confidently repeated her accusations? How could she bear to have Barbara know that Jamie was still lying to her about it? And, after all, she told herself dully, what did it matter?

For Cal's sake—surely not for her own—she knew that she would not be leaving and she was determined not to dwell on the whys and wherefores any longer.

Day after day passed and she did not see Jamie at all. Every evening he called the house, but he always talked to Max, using him to pass on news of Fitz's condition. Occasionally he would ask to speak to the children or even to Barbara, but Mary was never summoned to the phone. Any messages he had for her were relayed through Max. Generally they concerned the children's welfare. Only his first message had been directed to her personally, and that had been his terse command that she was not to come to the hospital again and that she could expect a discussion "of certain things" to be continued as soon as Fitz's condition stabilized. Max's face, when he had delivered that message, had been impassive

as usual, but even in his granite features had
been a glimmer of pity for the woman who had
ignited the boss's legendary temper.

Well, two could play at that game. From that
evening on, when the phone rang with Jamie's
seven o'clock call, Mary had already left the room.
He might not see her little act of rebellion, but at
least she had the satisfaction of knowing that she
was not pining by the phone, waiting for him to
relent and speak to her.

The nerve of the man, she fumed as she hid in
her room from the odious sound of the phone.
Again, with his convoluted male logic, he dared to
be angry with her for something he had done. He
was the betrayer, the liar; yet, when she had
caught him out, instead of admitting his guilt, he
had turned his anger on her. She was thinking just
that when there was a knock on her door.

"Mrs. Fitzhugh," Max's polite voice called
through the door, "you're wanted on the phone."

So at last the great man was condescending to
speak to her, was he? "Take a message, Max,"
she called back sweetly, "I can't come to the
phone right now."

"It's Mr. Fitzhugh, ma'am," he explained in a
gentle hint that she should rearrange her priori-
ties.

"Take a message," she repeated firmly, and
just for good measure turned the shower on
loudly in the bathroom. She heard his disapproving huff as his footsteps faded away.

Half an hour later she made a leisurely entrance
into the family room. The children were watching

a cowboy shoot-out on the TV, and Max was leafing through an outdoors magazine. She walked over to where he was sitting and waited.

"Did you want something, Mrs. Fitzhugh?"

She strove for an offhand, casual manner. "Was there a message for me?"

"No message, ma'am." His voice was matter-of-fact, but a muscle in his cheek twitched.

Her indifferent manner dissolved into impatience. "Surely he must have said something." No need to explain who "he" was.

"Not repeatable, ma'am." He could no longer control a rogue grin and buried his nose back into his magazine.

So, she had at least managed to goad him into a cuss word or two. The thought pleased her very much, and she gave herself an imaginary pat on the back as she strolled over to join the children.

Her eyes made another idle sweep of the room. "Where's Barbara this evening?"

"At the hospital with Mr. Fitzhugh," came Max's bland reply, and her good mood vanished.

Jamie would not allow her to go to the hospital, but he had sent for Barbara. When he had wanted someone to be with him, he had chosen her. She wanted to question Max further, but her damnable pride made her choke the words back.

"Would you like to play Scrabble, Max?" she said instead, reaching expectantly for the game board.

"No, ma'am," he surprised her with a polite refusal. "I doubt we'll have time."

Mary gave him a bewildered look; usually, he

was as anxious as she to while away the boring hours in a game or two. "I don't understand."

He seemed to be preoccupied, listening for something. In the distance they heard a car door slam. He rose quickly. "Come on, kids. Time for bed."

Two young voices wailed in unison that it was much too early, but he merely turned off the TV and took each by the hand, hurrying them past an open-mouthed Mary.

"Max, what on earth are you doing?"

He gave her another of his rare grins. "See you in the morning, ma'am—and good luck!" Tugging at the reluctant captives at the ends of his arms, he pulled them, protesting, out of the room with him.

While she was still trying to puzzle out his actions, the front door flew open and an irate Jamie slammed into the house.

"So there you are," he fumed.

Mary's first thought was that something had happened to Fitz and, because of her childish refusal to come to the phone, he had come to the house to deliver the bad news in person. She babbled her fears aloud, only to have him dismiss them with a curt gesture.

"Fitz is fine. You're the problem."

Her frantic imagination began to work overtime. He had just come from Barbara's arms and now he was going to tell her that he had decided to return to Barbara after all.

She had to know. "It's about Barbara, isn't it?" The words tumbled out.

"Yes," he admitted with a dark scowl, taking in her wan, thin face and troubled eyes. "She and I have been discussing you at some length."

"And now you're wondering how to break it to me," she guessed, heartsick at the thought. Awkwardly she moved away from him toward the hallway, anxious to put distance between herself and the words she did not want to hear.

It was comical in a sense. All the while she had been planning to forgive him—yes, like the stuffy prig he had accused her of being—he had been searching for a way to tell her he no longer wanted her. That was why he hadn't spoken to her all week. Being Jamie, he would naturally feel it necessary to deliver the killing blow in person—he was not the coward that she was.

Well, he might be strong enough to tell her that they were through, but she was not strong enough to stay and listen. Her steps quickened as she widened the distance between them, almost running now toward her room—that is, their room—no, his room. She couldn't even remember if the door had a lock on it, but she knew that the bathroom door did, so she set that as her confused goal, a refuge, a place to hide.

Ruthless arms cut off her escape and locked her frightened, desperate body tight against his. "You're through running away from me, Manya, and it's time you realized it. You and I are going to have a hell of a fight right now and you had damn well better prepare yourself to stand your ground and defend yourself as best you can, because I forbid you to run away from me ever again." His voice was hopelessly arrogant even as his hands soothed her trembling shoulders.

Mary looked up with bemused, wary eyes. "Don't try to let me down easily. Just let me go. Please."

Jamie's hands continued their soft stroking motions. "You are probably the most gullible, naive, trusting—no, change that to, nontrusting—insecure fool that ever lived. But I love you, as you damn well know by now, so I suppose I'll have to get used to your faults if we're going to spend the rest of our lives together."

"You love me?" she repeated in disbelief. "But I thought...that is, aren't you and Barbara...?"

He held her at arm's length with an exasperated sigh and set her down sternly in a nearby chair. "I repeat. Nontrusting, insecure—that's what you are. So, I am going to tell you one last time that I am not the father of Barbara's child, and this time, I expect you to believe me."

It seemed the most natural thing in the world to do when he looked at her like that, but still she hesitated. "B-Barbara, herself, told me," she said miserably.

He rubbed the back of his neck. "She lied. We had a long talk tonight at the hospital and she told me the whole story."

For the first time she began to believe that it might be possible. If only it were true. "But why would she make up such a story?" She was still skeptical.

"For what was apparently a very emotional and senseless female reason," he stated grimly, recalling the conversation. "She had just come from telling Fitz about the baby, hoping he would offer to marry her, and instead he insisted that she get an abortion or he would leave her. He spouted some nonsense about Cal being his only heir, and she was hurt and angry. When Barbara saw how happy we were in comparison, I guess she was irrationally jealous. She needed to strike out at someone, and you were just unfortunate enough to be there.

"She insists that when she had calmed down, she went to tell you that she had made the whole thing up, but by then you had gone, and she was afraid to tell Fitz or me what had made you leave."

Mary remembered vaguely Barbara's spiteful mutterings about being a storybook princess on that fateful day. It all made a twisted kind of sense.

"But she didn't get an abortion?" she probed, wanting to hear the entire story.

"No, she came to me, and I agreed to help her if she wanted to have the child and I promised her that Fitz wouldn't send either of them away. Then I proceeded to blackmail Dad into agreeing, although he was furious with her for disregarding his wishes. You know, in the back of his mind, he's always hoped that mother would eventually return to him, and he felt that if she learned about the baby, that would close the door to a reconciliation completely. And he was right."

"And does your mother know?" she questioned further, knowing from her own experience how devastating that information would be to her mother-in-law.

"Yes." His face was grim. "Barb's doing, I'm sure. She thought it would force a divorce, but of course Dad would not allow that. But it gave mother one more reason to hate him and therefore another reason for him to hate Barbara."

As if the explanation had exhausted him, he walked over to the liquor cabinet and poured himself a stiff drink, offering her one as well, which she refused with a wave of her hand. Picking up the squat tumbler of Scotch, he came back and sat beside her.

"Barbara is a complex creature—amoral and ruthless, but pitiable in a way. She does love Jaycie and, perhaps, Fitz as well, in her own cold way. However, I will admit that didn't stop her from making a pretty blatant pass at me when you first walked out. I guess she was desperate enough to settle for any port in a storm." At the numbed look that clouded Mary's eyes at this revelation, he immediately went on to clarify his meaning.

"I let her know in no uncertain terms that I wasn't having any of my father's leavings; and Dad let her down pretty brutally, too. However, she asked to stay on in spite of that. That's what I meant about being pitiable—staying on where she had been so coldly rejected. However, for Jaycie's sake, we all learned to live with the situation, if not with each other. Perhaps if I had known at the time she was also responsible for breaking up my own marriage, I wouldn't have been so generous.

I'm sure that's why she never confessed to her part in your leaving.''

Mary's head was reeling from trying to take in everything he had told her. Only one fact was really important: he had not had an affair with Barbara. She had sacrificed four years of her life for nothing. "What's going to happen now?''

"Well, I've been trying unsuccessfully for three years to convince Dad not to blame Jaycie for his troubles with Mother, but I guess he couldn't bear to put the blame where it really belonged— on his many infidelities. It was easier to blame Jaycie. You've seen how cruelly he's treated her, even refusing to have her in the same room with him. But this attack seems to have opened his eyes to his own failings. He's finally accepted the fact that the blame was all his and now he is determined to make it up to Jaycie.

"That's what that swarm of attorneys was all about last week. He's finally admitting paternity and his first concern now is getting to know his daughter.''

"When he's released from the hospital next week, he and Barb and Jaycie, along with our very good friend Mrs. Wright, are going on a long cruise so that Dad can recuperate and make friends with Jaycie at the same time.

"Are they going to be married, then?'' Everything else seemed to be working out exactly as Barbara wished it.

Jamie finished his drink before answering. "Unfortunately, that's one prize that will always elude Barb. The Fitzhughs truly do not divorce"—was

there a warning in his words? —"but she seems
more than willing to resume their old relationship.
And if that's what it takes to help Dad get to know
Jaycie better, then I'm all for it."

His restless hand went to the back of his neck
again. "All of which satisfies your curiosity, but
has nothing to do with us," he said menacingly.

Mary realized that he was in earnest about quar-
reling with her and he was not about to be put off
any longer. Still, she was deliriously happy. He
was not Barbara's lover and he loved her. She was
in seventh heaven and could not imagine what
there was left to quarrel about.

She had underestimated her opponent. The in-
flexible steel-gray of his eyes told her she still had
a lot of explaining of her own to do.

"You ran out on me, Manya, on the flimsiest of
evidence and without giving me a chance to defend myself," he accused bitterly.

"I left you a note," she reminded him with a
brief show of spirit. "I waited for you to come
after me and explain, but you never did."

His eyes darkened. "I never found any note.
Perhaps our friend Barb got to it first. But that
doesn't excuse you for running off with the first
man you met. When I finally traced you and discovered you were living with another man, I had
to force myself to stay away or I would have killed
you both. I told myself I was well rid of a cheating
tramp."

She wanted to reach across the space between
them and touch him, but he looked so forbidding
that she dared not. She knew what it cost him to

make that admission when only minutes ago he had told her that he still loved her.

"But I'm not. Truly I'm not. I've wanted to explain to you so many times about that," she began falteringly, "but somehow the timing was never right. It wasn't what you thought at all. That 'other man' was my brother." Despite the look of incredulity on his face, she went on to explain how Stan had returned to the country just at that time and how she had turned to him for help and he had taken her in.

She could see that he wanted to believe her, but now it was his turn to be doubtful. "It's no use. Your brother's name is John. John Karras. Don't you think I know that the man you were living with was Stanley Templeton?" He was once again the ruthless attorney breaking down the testimony of a hostile witness.

"I can explain," she continued hurriedly. "Karras was my father's name, but Stash, that is, Stan, I mean John, was mother's son by her first marriage and his father's last name was Templeton. He never changed it. His first name is Stanley. For some foolish reason Dad used to taunt him because Mom liked to call him Stash, and when he left home, he preferred to use his second name. Mostly I try to refer to him as John, but I guess childhood habits die hard. Even though I told you his name was John, when I think about him, I think of him as either Stan or Stash."

"But why didn't you tell me this when I accused you?—God, Manya, the things I accused you of," he groaned, pulling her into his lap and holding her close.

She snuggled up to him comfortably—home at last. "At first I thought I hated you, and it didn't make any difference to me what you thought of me; and then, I just couldn't bear to talk about it because it was all tied up with your leaving me, I thought, for Barbara. Eventually, I'm sure we would have straightened it out." She raised her lips up impatiently for his kiss. Why did he have to talk so much?

His hands smoothed her hair away from her face for agonizing minutes of delay and then traced her lips. If he didn't kiss her soon, she would bite the very fingers that were driving her wild. However, before she could put her threat into action, his brooding mouth came down on hers, his tongue finding its way past her parted lips to set her mouth afire. Her arms stole around his neck, drawing him even closer as her body molded itself to his demands.

At length he lifted his head lazily, allowing her to catch a breath. "And there's been no one else at all since you left me?" he demanded thickly. The question seemed to answer itself as she pressed herself to him, but he needed the words. "Has there?" he asked again, impatiently.

Was there still a trace of distrust in that passion-ridden voice? She remembered his words about fighting and learning to defend herself. "And if there had been?" she challenged gently.

"I would hate it," he gritted against her ear, his velvet tongue ceasing its delicate probing, but"—

he took a deep, defeated breath—"that wouldn't make me let you go. I need you too much," he confessed, allowing her once again to see his vulnerability where she was concerned.

Mary was sorry she had teased him. For some reason he was taking the matter entirely too seriously. He still held her on his lap, but almost at arm's length. "I had no right even to ask you that," he groaned, his face bleak. "I went wild after you left me, Manya. I took women like aspirins to relieve the pain—but they had no faces, no names—and when I was done with them, I still ached for what I had lost."

Jamie gave a weary, mocking laugh. "So you see, you still have every right to hate me, and I have no right at all to complain if you had taken a dozen lovers."

She couldn't bear to see him torturing himself like this. He had been hurt and he had behaved as a man betrayed by love will act. But it was all in the past now. If only she had trusted him in the beginning, none of it would have happened. She slid past the barricade of his stiff arms and pressed herself to him. "I have had only one lover," she said tremulously, "and I will love him forever— and after that."

His gray eyes were molten as he watched her. "And I've loved only one woman," he assured her.

Mary sighed blissfully, and a hand went up to circle the gold chain that was always around her neck. "Is our fight over, then?" she said, mimicking words he had once spoken to her.

"You know it is, because this time you've gotten your way."

"Good. I suppose we should kiss and make up, but I have a better idea." Her grin grew impudent as she pulled him out of the chair. "Let's go to bed and we'll see if we can't make that ache go away."

Epilogue

Mary was sitting by the pool at a table shaded from the hot afternoon sun by a huge gaily colored umbrella. Her back was toward him and her head was bent low over the notebook on which she was scratching away industriously. Even though her face was hidden from him, he could visualize the tiny frown lines of concentration around the corners of her mouth as she worked. The graceful curve of her neck seemed curiously vulnerable under the cloud of blond hair that was primly gathered in the French twist that she wore when she was preparing for a public appearance as the Congressman's lady.

He had mixed emotions about the hair style. He really did not like it; yet, in a perverse way, it pleased him that it concealed from others the silken glory that he knew so intimately.

He announced his presence with a slow kiss on the nape that he had been contemplating so lovingly. She flicked his touch away with an impatient gesture as she turned to face him, but her eyes widened in pleasure even as she pursed her lips in mock annoyance.

"What on earth are you doing home? Everything here is still a mess. I haven't even started to unpack, and there is nothing in the house to eat, unless it's thawed, and I haven't thawed anything. I thought you were going to take the children and Jan over to the old house to visit Fitz while I tried to get organized around here? And, frankly, I was hoping you would beg a meal for the lot of you while you were at it."

They had only arrived from Washington this morning, and as usual Mary was annoyed with herself for not having everything perfectly under control. She was determined to be the perfect politician's wife, regardless of anything Jamie could say to convince her to the contrary. Lord knows he had told her often enough that he liked her best disorganized, disheveled, and disrobed.

With a lazy smile at that last thought he slipped out of his suit jacket and loosened his tie. "I left Cal and the baby with Jan at Dad's. Jaycie has arrived for the summer, so Cal was more than anxious to stay behind to talk to her; and she and Dad insisted I leave the baby there, as well. Jan said she could manage without me—she had the baby cooing prettily for Fitz when I left—so, I thought I would come back to see how you were managing."

Jamie cast a slow glance around the premises, surprised to see that they were obviously alone. "Where's Mrs. Barnes? Surely she's around somewhere, setting things in order?"

Mary gave an uncomfortable wiggle in her chair. "Well, actually, she isn't here." Before Jamie could register a protest, she hurried on. "She called just after you left and asked if we could do without her for a few days. Her son is here from Wichita for the Fourth of July holiday, and they're planning a family reunion."

"And, of course, you told her that we could," he guessed with a despairing shrug.

"Well, yes." Her soft, smooth hand reached across the table to cover his, and the faint stirrings of irritation at how easily she allowed herself to be taken advantage of vanished. Just the sight of those hands made whole again, by the plastic surgery he had insisted upon, instilled him with a tenderness toward her that was overwhelming. And her soft, coaxing voice soothed him further.

"We can manage easily. Mrs. Barnes has stocked the freezer and the house is immaculate. Actually, it will be nice having the house and the children completely to ourselves for a few days. Jan is marvelous with the baby, and I'm still a rather good cook. And"—she cast a disbelieving glance at the comfortable sprawl of his long body in the chair—"if you really want to help, you can start by bringing the suitcases up to the bedrooms."

He sighed. "Okay, but there's really no hurry, is there? I thought I could take you out to lunch someplace."

"No, really, Jamie, I'm too busy." She turned back to study the copious notes before her.

He stared at her indulgently and leaned over to remove his shoes and socks, wiggling his freed toes comfortably. His speech for the Fourth of July was written, and later he would go over it with her one more time, but for the moment he had nothing better to do than relax and look at her.

True to his promise, he had built her a new house, in the pleasant suburb of Red Bridge, which pleased his constituents, his wife, and himself. It was situated on a large wooded lot with plenty of room for children and dogs, and its abundant acreage provided privacy and a calm serenity that was the perfect antidote to the Washington rat race. Taking a deep breath of the clean, sweet-smelling air, Jamie allowed himself to fall under its spell, reveling in the unaccustomed freedom from routine, like a child playing hookey.

But like a child, he wanted someone to play with, and watching Mary working so industriously when he had decided to goof off was not at all the way he planned to spend the rest of the afternoon.

"What are you doing?" He broke the silence plaintively.

"I'm being a dutiful wife," she retorted, recognizing his mood with some exasperation. "I'm making lists. Grocery lists. Shopping lists. Lists of all the people that we owe an invitation to while we're here. Lists of all the service people that Mrs. Barnes hasn't contacted yet. As you can see, the pool man has already been here, but our previous gardener has retired and I need to get someone else; and Mrs. Barnes has left me a note that the air conditioner may need Freon. I have menus to plan, etc., etc., etc." She frowned at him.

"And isn't my name on any of those lists?" His gray eyes returned her indignant glare with an injured innocence.

Mary closed her notebook with a martyred air. "I just knew you would be like this," she accused. "You always are when we get away from Washington. That's why I was hoping to get this out of the way before you got back. What on earth are you doing here so early? Didn't you and Fitz have anything to talk about? You haven't seen each other for months."

"Well, we did talk about Barb." He watched his wife's face for a reaction, and was not surprised to see the withdrawn look that still came over her features when the name was mentioned. She still had not forgiven Barb for separating them and neither had he.

"It seems Jaycie will be here the entire summer, rather than the three weeks originally agreed upon. Barb is on her honeymoon with her new husband."

At last he had her full attention. "Husband?"

They were both remembering that the cruise that Fitz had taken two years ago with Barbara had not led to the great reunion that Barb had been expecting. When it became evident that Fitz's only concern was for Jaycie, Barbara had accepted his offer of a very large financial settlement and a lavish apartment on the Plaza. They agreed that Jaycie would continue to live with her mother, with the proviso that Fitz should have unlimited access to his daughter. As it turned out, the money enabled Barbara to indulge her newfound taste for exotic travel, and Jaycie spent more time with Fitz than she did with her mother, under the expert care of the gray-haired housekeeper who also looked after Fitz.

"Husband," Mary repeated incredulously. "Someone obscenely wealthy, no doubt."

Jamie laughed. "Would you believe poor as a church mouse and fifteen years younger than Barb? It would appear that Barbara is a victim of her own game. Thanks to Dad's largesse, she and her husband are now enjoying life under the palm trees in Hawaii, and Jaycie is here for the summer and possibly the school term as well, if Dad has his way about it. He's decided it's high time that he had custody of Jaycie, and Barb was the one with the visitation rights. And I think her new husband is working to convince her along the same lines."

"But will Fitz be able to manage with a child in the house full time? Mrs. Gerron is a jewel, but that is asking a lot of her."

"Don't waste any time feeling sorry for Fitz. That old reprobate tried to steal Jan away from under my very nose. You'd think he'd know by now that Jan is more like your sister than little Helene's nanny. But Jan did take pity on him and promised to send a friend of hers over to see him; and, of course, for the summer Jaycie will be with us most of the time, anyway."

He took the notebook out of Mary's protective hands and tossed it carelessly into an empty chair as he talked.

"By the way, Dad is just crazy about Helene.

She crawled right into his arms without a murmur. He ate it up. Naming her after mother has really made her special to him. Oh, and another news flash. Mom is coming down in a couple of weeks to meet her namesake.''

Mary's eyes widened. "Your mother's coming here? To Kansas City? When did she tell you that?"

"She didn't. Dad did. It seems they've kept in touch since his illness. And when he told her we were going to be here for the summer, she decided to pay her grandchildren a visit. She'll be staying with us, of course; but even so, coming to Kansas City is such a concession for her, that Dad is quite optimistic about a possible reconciliation."

Mary shook her head cautiously. "I hope he won't be disappointed." They were silent for a moment, both of them wanting everyone—especially Fitz and Helene—to be as happy as they were, but remembering how far apart his parents had grown over the years.

"They'll work it out," Jamie assured her. "We did." His hand moved to caress her cheek.

Mary cast a furtive glance in the direction of her notebook. Jamie's hand moving to brush her hair told her it was a hopeless task, but she tried anyway. "I really have a lot of work to do, Jamie."

His hands continued their gentle stroking.

"You'll muss my hair," she protested weakly. "It took Mr. Ray a precious hour of my time this morning to set it. He calls it my campaign coiffure," she remembered with a grin.

His hand slipped down to her throat and played

with the gold chain around her neck before slipping lower to trace the neckline of her dress. "Pretty dress," he murmured approvingly.

"Yes, and it cost you a fortune." Her fingers touched his, trying to still their sensuous wanderings. "Stop that. I thought you were going to unpack those suitcases."

He thought about it a minute and then, as if in agreement, he started to unbutton his shirt. For a moment Mary thought he was preparing himself to do just that, but the warm glint in his eyes told her a different story.

"Nooooo," she wailed. "I have a million things to do." Her hand went to his shirt, trying to stop him from undoing it.

The movement caused his gray eyes to rest on the tiny gold watch on her wrist. He lifted her hand and kissed the pulse that was pounding rapidly just below the thin gold band of the watch.

"When I bought you this watch for Christmas, did I remember to tell you that it was waterproof?" he remarked almost absently as he rubbed his lips roughly against the sensitive skin.

"What has that to do with any—" Her eyes widened in comprehension as the workings of her husband's mind became clear to her. "No, Jamie," she half begged, half laughed. "You can't. My hair...my new dress..."

"Tsk, tsk, sweetheart," he chided as he took his wallet out of his pocket and laid it carefully on the table between them. "Once you accused me of being a stuffed shirt. We wouldn't want to say the same thing about you, would we? Although, I must admit, your shirt is stuffed much more enticingly than mine ever was." He slipped out of that shirt with little effort and turned to grasp his wife by the elbows, drawing her to her feet.

"Tell me again you love me, sweetheart," he coaxed against her throat.

"Of course I love you." Her voice broke in a husky whisper. "B-but I just don't want *to* love you at this exact m-moment," she stammered, trying to still the betraying flush that was sweeping across her body.

"You will," he promised as he pushed her gently into the pool.

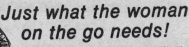
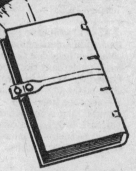

Share the joys and sorrows of real-life love with
Harlequin American Romance!™